GOAL II

LIVING THE DREAM

ROBERT RIGBY

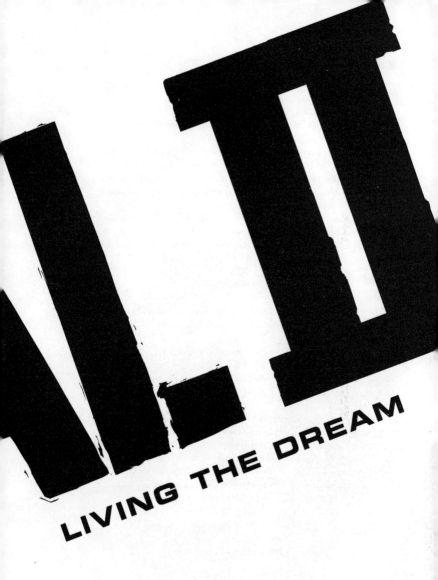

LIVING THE DREAM

HARCOURT, INC.

Orlando   Austin   New York   San Diego   Toronto   London www.HarcourtBooks.com

First published 2007 by Corgi Books/Random House Children's Books UK
First Harcourt paperback edition 2007

Library of Congress Cataloging-in-Publication Data
Rigby, Robert.
Goal II: living the dream/novelization
by Robert Rigby.—1st Harcourt paperback ed.
p.   cm.
Summary: After leaving Los Angeles to play soccer with Newcastle
United, Mexican American Santiago Muñez is recruited to play for
Real Madrid, one of the best teams in the world, and must struggle
with the pressure and temptations his newfound fame brings.
[1. Soccer—Fiction.   2. Fame—Fiction.   3. Conduct of life—Fiction.
4. Real Madrid Club de Fútbol—Fiction.   5. Mexican Americans—Fiction.
6. Spain—Fiction.]   I. Title.   II. Title: Goal two.
III. Title: Living the dream.
PZ7.R44177Gob   2007
[Fic]—dc22   2006019142
ISBN 978-0-15-205881-4

Text set in Sabon
Designed by April Ward

A C E G H F D B

Printed in the United States of America

ACKNOWLEDGMENTS FOR *GOAL II: LIVING THE DREAM*

GOAL II original story by Mike Jefferies and Adrian Butchart
GOAL II screenplay by Mike Jefferies, Adrian Butchart,
and Terry Loane
PRODUCERS Mike Jefferies, Matt Barrelle, and Mark Huffam
EXECUTIVE PRODUCERS Lawrence Bender, Jeff Abberley,
Julia Blackman, and Stuart Ford
COPRODUCERS Danny Stepper, Jo Burn, Raquel De Los Reyes,
and Henning Molfenter
ASSOCIATE PRODUCERS Allen Hopkins, Stevie Hargitay,
Nicolas Gautier, Steve McManaman, and Jonathan Harris

SPECIAL THANKS TO:
FIFA
Adidas
Real Madrid
UEFA Champions League
La Liga

1

Santiago effortlessly avoided a lunging tackle and closed on the goal.

The Newcastle faithful, a sea of black and white on all four sides of St. James' Park, roared their approval as Santiago brushed off a second challenge.

His eyes lifted for a split second and his brain made the instinctive and instant, computer-like calculation: range, trajectory, power.

And then, with hardly a break in stride, Santiago struck a perfectly weighted and flighted ball past the despairing dive of the keeper into the top corner of the net.

The crowd erupted, joyously celebrating what was to be voted the Premiership goal of the season as Santiago raised both arms to the sky in acknowledgment of their adulation.

The fans' roars thundered around the stadium, into the city streets, and down to the River Tyne.

And as Santiago stood, arms raised, the echoes of those cheers could be heard across Europe in a darkened room at the very heart of Spain.

A group of men, all expensively suited, were staring intently at Santiago's frozen image on a huge plasma screen.

They spoke softly, almost conspiratorially, in Spanish, as if they were afraid that unwanted listeners might overhear their words.

The electronic shutters on the windows slowly began to open and daylight spilled into the screening room, revealing a desktop cluttered with photographs, sheets of statistics, videocassettes, biographical notes, everything dedicated to the life and football career of one young man: Santiago Muñez.

The man at the center of the group turned to one of his colleagues. "Harris and Muñez played well together at Newcastle; maybe they would be good together here."

"Buy they play in the same position now," came the instant reply.

He nodded toward the plasma screen and within seconds the Muñez highlights reel was rolling again, cutting to a different match and a bustling run by Santiago that ended in another spectacular goal.

"Exactly," said the first man.

———

Santiago had grown to love Newcastle and its people, who had adopted him as an honorary "Geordie," which is how the locals were known.

It was a long way from his Mexican roots and just as distant from the run-down district of Los Angeles in California where he had grown up and developed his natural skills as a soccer player.

He would, almost certainly, have still been playing local league soccer, as they called it back home, had it not been for a chance encounter with Glen Foy.

Glen, an ex-Newcastle player himself and a one-time scout for the club, was on vacation in L.A. when he saw Santiago playing in a park match. He knew instantly he was watching someone special, someone blessed with footballing gifts granted to very few.

Against all the odds, Glen arranged a trial with Newcastle for Santiago, and what followed had since become part of the folklore of the famous Tyneside club.

Sometimes, even after a season and a half, it still seemed like a dream to Santiago—a dream come true.

He missed the sunshine of L.A. and he missed his grandmother, Mercedes, and his younger brother, Julio, but life in Newcastle had incredible compensations—the designer clothes, the top-of-the-line BMW, the beautiful new home.

And then, of course, there was Roz.

Roz was a nurse; they had met soon after Santiago arrived in Newcastle, and little more than a year later, they were planning their wedding.

Life was wonderful. It could hardly get better. Santiago had moved swiftly from park player to St. James' Park hero.

Fans of Newcastle United, collectively known as the Toon Army, knew he was a great, natural goal scorer, and many of the faithful predicted that someday he would challenge the scoring feats of even the legends, Jackie Milburn and Alan Shearer.

But, of course, that depended on the club being able to hang on to a player now regarded as one of the hottest properties in football.

2

THE BMW DREW TO A HALT in the wide driveway of the new house and Santiago switched off the engine and stepped from the vehicle.

He'd been for a run after training and had enjoyed every minute of it. Preseason was a time of mixed emotions, the huge anticipation of the campaign that was soon to begin and the frustration of counting off the days until the first Premiership match.

Santiago went into the house, pulled off his sweatshirt, walked past boxes still waiting to be unpacked, and decided he would get himself a drink before taking a shower.

As he entered the living room, heading for the kitchen, he saw Roz sitting on one of the expensive sofas they had recently bought. She was deep in conversation with a smartly dressed young man.

The young man was pointing out something of particular interest in a color brochure, and on the sofa and the nearby coffee table were various fabric swatches and color charts.

"Hi," said Santi as the young man looked up and smiled. Santiago didn't see Roz's frown as he continued into the kitchen and went to the fridge.

A few minutes later, as Santi downed another mouthful of orange juice, he heard the front door close.

Roz walked into the kitchen and she wasn't looking happy. "It's ten to five, Santi. The meeting with the wedding planner was at four."

Santiago's eyes widened as he realized exactly why he was in big trouble. "Roz, I'm sorry, I lost track of time . . ."

"We're supposed to decide on this stuff together."

Santiago smiled and shrugged his shoulders, going for the charm offensive, which usually worked. "What do I know about the color of the flowers and the menus? You decide; you're good at that. As long as you show up at the wedding I'll be happy, even if you're only wearing your nurse's uniform."

Roz shook her head and forced back a smile. She was used to Santiago's tactics. She lifted a hand and went to give him a playful slap but Santi grabbed her wrist and pulled her close.

"You Latin boys are so cheeky," said Roz, trying to push him away.

But Santiago wasn't giving up. He moved in for a kiss and then stepped back with a look of mock horror. "You wouldn't leave me at the altar, would you? You *are* going to turn up?"

"I might," said Roz, feigning complete indifference. "If you're lucky."

Santiago wrapped his arms around Roz and drew her closer. But before he could kiss her again, she put both hands on his chest and shoved him away.

"Go and have a shower. You stink."

Santiago laughed, but instead of going to the shower, he decided to check out the latest sports news. He picked up the remote and switched on the TV, where a report on Real Madrid's arrival in Tokyo for their annual preseason tour had just begun.

The entire first-team squad was making their way through the airport, as fans screamed and cameras flashed. They were all there: Beckham, Ronaldo, Roberto Carlos, Zidane, Casillas, Guti, all the superstars. And in the thick of it all, smiling, waving, loving every moment, was Gavin Harris.

"Look!" yelled Santiago to Roz. "It's Gavino!"

Roz raised her eyes to the heavens and didn't bother to even glance toward the TV.

But Santiago's eyes were glued to the screen. Gavin Harris was his friend, his buddy, and for a brief while, he had been his teammate at Newcastle.

Then Real had surprised the football world by swooping up Gavin. It was a major shock; Gavin was a terrific player—there was no doubt about that—but he wasn't getting any younger and he had a well-deserved reputation for enjoying a good time, which many pundits predicted could only shorten his career.

But Gavin had begun well and had scored his fair quota of goals. Then the goals started to dry up. And for a striker, goals were what counted.

Santiago and Roz were seated at the table in the Indian restaurant with Jamie Drew and his girlfriend, Lorraine, and Roz's mom, Carol.

Jamie was Santi's other good friend from his earliest days at Newcastle United. They had played in the reserves together as two hopefuls, but while Santiago's career had soared to dazzling heights, Jamie's had gone in completely the opposite direction.

One bad tackle in a reserve-team match had resulted in a shattered meniscus and a torn cruciate ligament in his right leg. It meant that he would never play professional football again.

But Jamie was a Liverpudlian and a born optimist; he usually managed to look on the bright side of life, and if there was ever a twinge of jealousy at Santiago's success, he never let it show.

Jamie was genuinely delighted that his friend had made it to the big time, and besides, he and Lorraine had their own reasons to be cheerful. Lorraine was eight months pregnant, and as the others studied the restaurant menu, she proudly pulled the latest ultrasound photograph of the baby from her handbag.

She passed the photograph to Roz, who looked at it and smiled.

Carol was more interested in the wine than in blurry images of unborn babies. "Time for a toast, I think." She raised her glass and looked at Santiago and Roz. "To your new home."

They drank the toast and then Lorraine turned to Santiago. "Will your granny be coming over for the wedding?"

"I wouldn't like to be the one who tries to stop her." Santiago smiled. "But she's going to need subtitles for Jamie's best man speech."

Jamie ignored the laughter and concentrated on the menu. "You going for the extra-hot vindaloo again, Santi?"

Santi nodded. "Sounds good to me."

"Oh, have a bit of consideration, Jamie," said Roz. "I'm the one who has to share a bed with him."

Santiago and Jamie were still laughing when they saw Glen Foy approaching the table.

"Hey, Glen," said Roz, indicating a spare chair. "Good timing, we're just ordering."

Glen didn't sit down. "No thanks, I had a late lunch." He looked at Santiago. "Can I have a word?"

"Sure, of course. Grab a chair."

Glen shook his head. "No, in private."

The restaurant kitchen was hardly private. Cooks were busy at sizzling pans and steaming pots, and waiters were gliding in and out, shouting orders and collecting dishes.

They were all far too busy to pay any attention to Glen and Santiago, who was standing like a rabbit frozen in a car's headlights, his eyes wide with amazement as he tried to take in what Glen had just told him.

"You *are* joking?"

"I wouldn't joke about this, Santi. I've been on the phone for hours."

Glen had never planned on being a footballer's agent. He ran a garage, specializing in restoring vintage cars, but when Santiago was offered his contract with Newcastle there was no one else he wanted as his representative. So Glen had taken the job, a little reluctantly. He wasn't a natural in the role; most agents were pushy, brash, outgoing, but he wanted the best for his young protégé, so he was giving it his best shot.

"They want to meet, Santi," he said. "But we have to keep this quiet, okay?"

Santiago nodded, still dazed at what Glen had told him.

The evening passed in a blur, Santiago hardly tasting the vindaloo. He sat at the table, only half hearing the conversation about babies and weddings and new homes, wanting to shout out what Glen had told him, but he knew he couldn't say a word.

He broke the news to Roz when they got back to the house. Roz tried to stay calm. She nodded, asked a few questions, and then decided that she, too, needed a few minutes to take in all the implications.

Santiago was sitting on the bed, still in a daze, when she emerged from the en suite bathroom, still brushing her teeth.

"But you're happy here," she said through a mouthful of toothpaste.

"I couldn't be happier," answered Santiago.

"And you've got two more years on your contract. You're not leaving Newcastle; the fans will go mad. You're the best player they've got."

3

REAL MADRID: the biggest, the richest, the most glamorous, the most successful football club on the planet.

Nine-time European champions, twenty-nine Spanish League titles, seventeen Spanish Cups, the UEFA Cup twice, the Spanish Super Cup seven times, the Intercontinental Cup three times. The glory list goes on and on.

The club and the players are constantly in the spotlight and in demand all over the world. They were playing Júbilo Iwata in Tokyo in a preseason friendly game as Santiago and Glen took their first breathtaking looks at the Ginza district of the city.

Rain was falling steadily, but the dazzling neon lights illuminated the night, highlighting the chic clubs, the futuristic architecture, and the swarming, heaving mass of humanity.

Santiago and Glen were in the back of a limousine that had collected them from the airport and was easing its way through lines of traffic toward the luxury Park Hyatt Hotel. A towering billboard, featuring an immaculately groomed David Beckham shaving with a Gillette razor, stood out among the mass of advertisements.

Glen saw Santiago looking nervously up at the billboard and smiled.

"Who knows?" he said.

The limo slid to a standstill outside the hotel, where more than a hundred Madrid fans were waiting, beneath umbrellas and with cameras at the ready, for the return of their heroes from the Júbilo match. Most of them had been there for hours and would happily wait for many more just to catch a close-up glimpse of one of *los galácticos,* as the superstar players were nicknamed.

As Santi and Glen emerged from the limo, many of the waiting crowd turned to look, but only a few bothered to snatch a quick photograph.

Santiago and Glen hurried through the rain to the hotel entrance, where a smiling, expensively dressed man was waiting. "Welcome, Mr. Muñez, and Mr. Foy. My name is Leo Vegaz, player liaison." He looked up at the teeming rain. "I personally arranged the weather so you would feel at home."

They were swiftly checked in to the hotel and shown to their suites. It had been a long, tiring flight, but Santiago was wide-awake and alive with nervous energy. This was all happening so quickly and suddenly.

He grabbed a quick shower and emerged, wrapped in just a towel. On the huge plasma TV, the highlights of the Real match were being shown. Santiago smiled at the skills being displayed by the *galácticos* as he moved over to a freshly made tray of sushi, sitting on a tabletop. It looked good, and Santi realized that he was hungry, but before he could pick up one of the delicate mouthfuls, the room telephone rang.

Santiago hurried across to the phone and picked up the receiver.

It was Glen, and he didn't waste his words. "They want to see us."

Santiago could see himself in one of the room's mirrors, naked apart from the towel wrapped around his waist. "What, *now*?" he said.

Santiago's suite was cool but the presidential suite was something else. The decor and furnishings were black, ultramodern, and minimalist, and the floor-to-ceiling windows gave a panoramic view of Tokyo.

Leo Vegaz had escorted Santiago and Glen into the suite, where one man was standing by the windows, looking out over the city. He turned as he heard the door to the room open and walked toward Santi with his hand outstretched. "Rudi Van Der Merwe," he said. "I'm the club coach."

"Yes, I know," said Santi as they shook. "Pleased to meet you."

Glen held out his own right hand to the Madrid coach. "Mr. Van Der Merwe, it's a pleasure. I'm honored to shake your hand, sir."

Van Der Merwe nodded modestly and then looked at Santi. "You've come a long way at short notice. Do you think you're ready for Real Madrid, Muñez?"

Santiago had no chance to reply. The door opened and two men entered. One was instantly recognizable to almost anyone in the world of football. It was Florentino Pérez, the president of the world's most famous club.

Leo Vegaz was ready to make the introductions. "Gentlemen," he said to Santi and Glen, "may I introduce our president, Señor Pérez, and the club's director of football, Señor Burruchaga."

"Thank you for coming," said Pérez, looking directly at Santi.

Glen was determined to make all the right noises and to extend the correct courtesies. "We're very happy to be here. Thanks for bringing us over."

Pérez nodded to Glen, but he was very obviously

focused on the player. "How was your trip over, Santiago?" he asked in Spanish.

"Fine, thanks," replied Santi, also in Spanish. "It's great to be here."

Leo Vegaz gestured to the comfortable-looking sofas grouped around a low coffee table and all six men sat down.

The introductions were over and Burruchaga was ready to get down to business. "We've been watching you play," he said to Santi. "You had an impressive last season."

Santiago shrugged. "I'm just part of a great team."

Señor Pérez nodded, identifying immediately with Santiago's sentiments about being part of a great team. "Real Madrid is unique in the world of football. We demand total dedication. We pride ourselves on being the ultimate exponents of the beautiful game. We want to offer our followers the ultimate football experience."

Santiago listened intently to every word. He knew full well that Señor Pérez had probably said the same words many times when talking about his beloved club, but that didn't make the sentiments any less impressive.

The six men were sizing each other up, making assessments, particularly Van Der Merwe, but Burruchaga was the one wanting to push the meeting on;

as far as he was concerned, discussion over football philosophy could come later.

"With the World Cup next year, many players are on the move," he said, looking at Santi. "And we want you, Santiago. We're confident that we can make this work."

Santiago turned to Glen; it was moving even faster than he had imagined and there were still so many questions to be answered.

Of course he wanted to play for Real Madrid; who in their right mind wouldn't? But Santiago wanted to *play* football, and the way Michael Owen had spent much of the previous season warming the Real Madrid substitutes' bench had entered his thoughts many times since he had heard of Real's interest.

Owen was one of the best strikers in world football, so where might that leave him? But Santi knew that however good a player was, sometimes a transfer just didn't work out. The Real delegation obviously believed he could fit into their system and he had to keep believing in his own ability to play at the highest level. And a day can be a long time in football, and in the destiny of its star players, as Santiago would soon discover.

"We have to act quickly," said Burruchaga. "The transfer window closes at midnight tomorrow."

———

The nine-hour time difference between Newcastle and Tokyo was doing nothing to help Santiago communicate with Roz. And not only that, Roz's duties as a nurse meant that she couldn't just leave her cell phone switched on to take calls whenever she wanted.

Santi had left text and voice-mail messages but, so far, there had been no response. And he had to make a decision. Almost immediately.

He walked back into the bar of the Park Hyatt Hotel, where Glen was sitting staring at two ice-cold beers. Santi shook his head as he sat on the stool. "I left another message."

As they reached for their beers, a familiar, friendly voice boomed into their ears and Gavin Harris wrapped one arm around them both. "All right, ladies?"

Santiago laughed; Gavin almost always made him laugh.

"Gavino!" he said, standing up to hug his old friend.

Gavin turned to Glen and they shook hands and then Gavin gestured to the bartender for another beer. "You'll hate Madrid," he said to Santi. "No snow, no rain, no mud. And they all speak Spanish!"

Glen spoke urgently but quietly; all this was meant to be a secret. "We haven't said yes yet!"

"What are you, mental?" said Gavin eyeballing Glen's modest suit and speaking loudly enough for almost everyone in the bar to hear. "With your ten percent you could splash out a bit. Get yourself a new suit, maybe even a full makeover."

Glen was used to Gavin's sense of humor. "Just what I've always dreamed of."

Santiago took a sip of his beer. "It's a big decision, Gavino. Roz and I just got this great new house, and—"

"House!" said Gavin, interrupting. "Are you trying to tell me you came halfway round the world for a night of karaoke? No one says no to Real Madrid."

Santiago knew that Gavin was right; even with the fears that he could find himself spending matches on the bench like Owen, it would be crazy to turn down an opportunity like this, an opportunity that would probably never come again. If he rejected Real Madrid now, the club would be unlikely to come knocking at his door a second time.

He was thinking over Gavin's words as Van Der Merwe and Burruchaga entered the bar and walked over to them.

Van Der Merwe smiled at Santi and Glen and then checked his watch before giving Gavin a look that was loaded with meaning.

"I'm just trying to put him off, boss," said Gavin, grinning guiltily. "We've got enough kids on the squad."

"It is a big decision," said Van Der Merwe to Santi. "Very tempting. All that money."

"I just wish I had more time."

"Ah, the transfer deadline," said Burruchaga. "It helps to focus the mind. In these matters, I have one foolproof tactic. Listen to your heart, then listen to your head. And when you have listened to your heart and your head, do exactly as your wife tells you."

The old joke raised a few polite laughs, even from Gavin; after all, Burruchaga was Real Madrid's director of football.

But Santiago hardly managed a smile. He still had a life-changing decision to make—and he hadn't yet spoken to Roz.

4

THE NEWSPAPER BACK PAGES were screaming the
headline:

OWEN JOINS NEWCASTLE

After weeks of speculation, rumor, and denials,
there had been talk of his moving back to Liverpool,
or to Chelsea, or Arsenal, or even to one of the Ital-
ian giants, but finally the deal was done and the news
was out; after just one season with Real Madrid,
Michael Owen was returning to the Premiership with
Newcastle United.

It was no great surprise that Owen should choose
to leave Real; a player of his international standing
could never be content to spend so much time warming the bench, waiting to make cameo appearances.

And even though his goals-per-minutes-on-the-field ratio had been higher than any striker in La Liga, everyone knew that it was only a matter of time before he moved on. But Newcastle was a shock choice, and now the rumor mill was spinning again as the press, pundits, supporters, and even players wondered what it meant for the other strikers at the club.

The sports journalists and fans were out in force at Newcastle Airport when Santiago and Glen finally made it back from Tokyo. Questions were fired like bullets as they moved through the crowd toward a waiting car.

"Is it true, Santi?"

"Are you leaving Newcastle?"

"Have you signed for Real?"

Santiago just smiled and stayed silent while Glen did his best to give noncommittal answers, trying to say nothing, but in fact, saying everything.

Santiago knew that Roz was back at the house, waiting, and he was anxious to get there so that they could talk things over.

When he stepped from the car and walked toward the house, he was welcomed by two engineers, working from the basket of the hoist on the top of their white van. They were adjusting the satellite dish on the wall of the house as the radio in the van blared out more on the debate over Santi's future now that Michael Owen had arrived.

"Hey, Santi," shouted one of them as Santiago approached. "You're not leaving us, are you?"

Santiago said nothing, but as he went into the house and into the living room, he saw immediately that the TV was switched on; yet more coverage on the Michael Owen signing and his "unveiling" at St. James' Park.

The TV pictures showed Owen looking a little bewildered but smiling broadly as he shook hands with the manager and club chairman and then proudly held up the famous black-and-white shirt that already bore his name. And the coverage finally confirmed one of football's worst-kept secrets: Santiago Muñez was moving in the opposite direction, to Real, on a two-year contract.

The story was everywhere; there was no escaping it.

And there was no escaping Roz's anger as she emerged from the kitchen and gave Santiago no chance to speak. "How could you do this without talking to me?"

"I had to make a decision," said Santi. "I couldn't get through to you."

Outside, the two satellite dish engineers could hear Roz's raised voice and were hoping that maybe they might learn, firsthand, exactly what had happened in Tokyo. One of them lowered the basket a little so that they could peer through the window as Santiago continued with his excuses.

"I tried to call. On your cell phone, here at the house."

"You could have waited! Asked for more time! I'm your fiancée, for God's sake!"

Roz grabbed her coat. She was due to leave for work and as far as she was concerned there was nothing more to say. She stormed out of the house, slamming the front door and glaring at the two men in the basket as she stomped toward her car.

They smiled sheepishly and watched as Roz drove away.

"That could have gone better," said one of them as he began to raise the basket again.

Santiago waited until the evening before going to see Roz at the hospital. She was on the night shift and Santi reckoned that if he arrived later at the ward, they might be able to talk because most of the patients would have been settled down for the night.

He was right. He entered the ward and saw the other duty nurse, who recognized Santi instantly and nodded to a small, side ward. "She's in there."

Santiago gently pushed open the door and looked through. Roz was checking the pulse of an elderly patient called Mr. Ives. He was a regular in the ward, with a long-term medical condition that needed frequent monitoring. And he knew Santiago well.

"Oh, here he is," he said as Santiago stepped nervously into the room. "The git who's stealing my beautiful Rosalind away from me. You're in the bad books today, son."

Santiago didn't need to be told that, and Roz wasn't making it any easier for him as she kept her eyes on her patient. "You save your breath, Mr. Ives."

Mr. Ives looked at Santiago, waiting for him to continue, mischievously enjoying his obvious discomfort.

"You might think that this is easy for me," said Santiago.

Roz still wasn't looking at Santi, but Mr. Ives was watching him flounder as he searched for the words.

"I love you, Roz, and I want to marry you. None of that changes. But right now, before we have kids, responsibilities, we can go places, do things, just you and me."

Roz saw Mr. Ives's eyes switch to her as he waited for her response. She spoke without turning back to Santi. "I don't understand what you're asking. Are you saying you want me to come and live with you in Spain? I'm not sure I want to live in Spain, Santi. I love Newcastle."

"I love it, too. This town has been good to me. If I hadn't come here, I wouldn't have found the most important thing in my life . . . *you.*"

Mr. Ives smiled and nodded at Roz. "He's got a point there, love."

"But what about our house?" said Roz almost as if she were asking the question of Mr. Ives. "And the wedding? And my mum, and my job? I've got my exams at Easter."

"You can come and see me on your days off. I'll fly back when I can. Roz, I can't walk away from this chance. This is my life, and I want you there with me."

Slowly Roz turned to look at Santiago. "But I can't even speak Spanish."

"I'll teach you," said Santi with a smile.

Roz was melting. She smiled as Santiago moved closer but was still determined to have the final word. "I'm not eating paella."

Santiago laughed out loud and then wrapped his arms around Roz and kissed her.

Mr. Ives was smiling, too. As Santiago glanced in his direction, he beckoned him over to his bedside.

The young footballer let go of his fiancée and went to Mr. Ives. "Do us a favor, lad," he said almost in a whisper, making Santi lean closer so that he could hear. "If you see that Gavin Harris fella, tell him he's *shite*!"

5

A NEW SIGNING for Real Madrid always sparked more than just interest in the city. It ignited the love, the passion, and the obsession for football and for the club felt by the majority of Madrid's people.

The press conference hastily arranged to mark Santiago's signing was being avidly watched on television screens throughout Spain—but almost everywhere in Madrid.

In hotels and bars, in hospitals and residential homes, in garages and fire stations, even in the city prison, people clustered around TVs to get their first look at the new boy.

Santi had just been presented with his team shirt and was smiling for the regulation photographs.

"Now that I'm here, I just want to play football," he said in answer to a reporter's question.

The reporter came straight back. "Do you think you'll get much first-team action?"

Before Santi could answer, his new coach, Rudi Van Der Merwe, was quick to reply. "As you all know, at Real we have the best strikers in the world. The competition is fierce. No player wants to sit on the bench and Santiago is no different."

Roz was sitting at the back of the room and her smile was almost as broad and as proud as Santiago's as he became a Real Madrid player.

But Real is not the only famous football club in Spain's capital city; there is also Atlético de Madrid. And while Atlético has never reached the dazzling heights of its more illustrious neighbor, it still also has its own history, its tradition, and its fanatical followers.

In a run-down bar in one of the poorer quarters of the city, where old Atlético pennants and faded match posters decorated the tobacco-stained walls, the Real conference was being watched on an ancient TV set by the few customers nursing their beers.

The regulars watched with a mixture of disdain and envy; Real could afford the players their own club could only ever dream of signing.

There was a close-up shot of Santiago as he expressed his genuine joy at the move. "I couldn't be happier. Since I was a kid I always dreamed of playing for Real."

In the barroom, an attractive woman in her mid-forties, standing behind the bar, stared at the TV screen as though she had seen a ghost.

One of the customers drained his glass and placed it on the bar top. "Another beer, please, Rosa."

The woman did not move; she did not even hear him. She just kept staring at the face on the television screen.

The elderly customer turned away from the bar and looked over to where another man was perched on a stepladder, as he replaced a fluorescent light strip. "Hey, Miguel," called the customer, "your wife is eyeing the young men again."

"Rosa-Maria," snapped the man on the stepladder. "Another beer for José, please."

The startled woman reacted as though she had been woken from a dream. But she quickly regained her composure and reached for the empty beer glass, forcing herself not to snatch another look at the television screen.

In one corner of the room, a group of scruffy young teenagers were clustered around a foosball table, shouting noisily each time a goal was scored.

"Enrique," called Miguel from his stepladder. "You done your homework?"

A wiry and unkempt-looking thirteen-year-old glanced up from one end of the table. "I'll do it later."

"You'll do it *now*!" said Miguel. The new fluorescent strip was installed and Miguel stepped down onto the floor. "And you lot," he shouted to the other kids. "Get out! Go home!"

The kids knew better than to argue and they departed with mutters and surly looks as Enrique glared at his father and headed off to begin his homework.

Madrid was going to take a lot of getting used to, for both Santiago and Roz.

The following morning they kissed good-bye on the steps of their hotel on the Calle de Zurbano before setting off on their own journeys of discovery.

For Santiago it was day one of training, his first visit to the incredible new training complex on the edge of the city, and his first meeting with the rest of the squad.

For Roz it was day one of getting to know the city, the place which—if all went according to plan— would be her home before too long.

By the time Santiago arrived at the space-age training ground, his nervousness had grown to acute anxiety. He stepped from the car and felt a familiar tightness in his chest, which usually meant he needed a hit from his asthma inhaler.

He took the inhaler from his pocket, breathed the chemicals deep into his lungs, and immediately felt better. As he slipped the inhaler back into his jacket pocket, he heard the expensive purr of a powerful engine and stopped to watch as a silver Bentley pulled into the parking area.

Gavin Harris was at the wheel, all smiles, all style, radiating success. He got out of the car, took off his sunglasses, and grinned at Santiago. Words were not necessary; this really was a different world.

They walked toward the changing rooms together, past a group of young kids who stood peering through the barrier fence. A few of them called out to Gavin and he waved an acknowledgment. Among the watchers was Enrique, the thirteen-year-old from the rundown bar.

Gavin enjoyed describing some of the delights of Spanish living that awaited his friend as they changed for training. But Santiago was hardly listening; he was focused on making a good impression on the coaching staff and his new teammates once the session got under way.

The sun was beating down as they walked toward the training fields. Players were beginning gentle warm-ups under the watchful eyes of the coaching staff, including former Liverpool and Real star Steve McManaman.

Macca, as he was known throughout the sport,

had been a great favorite with the Real supporters, the Madridistas, during his time at the Bernabéu Stadium, playing a leading part in two successful European campaigns. When he retired from playing, Coach Van Der Merwe had been quick to snap him up as an assistant trainer, deciding that his experience would be invaluable for the present squad.

The *galácticos* were in a group together. Some of the most famous names in football—Raúl, Zidane, Roberto Carlos, Ronaldo, and David Beckham—were easing their way into the session, chatting, laughing, supremely confident.

Santiago had briefly met Beckham once before, in a London bar after his Newcastle debut against Fulham. The world's most famous footballer had watched the match during a brief visit to the U.K. to shoot a commercial, and afterward he had sought out Santiago to offer his congratulations.

When Santi told him that he was a Real Madrid fan, Beckham had said to him, "Carry on playing like that, you'll be there one day."

And now he was. He was a Real Madrid player. It was still hard to believe, but it was true.

He stood back, self-consciously, watching Gavin high-five the other players and wondering if Beckham would remember their brief encounter.

Then the English captain turned toward him, smiled his famous smile, and held out his hand in welcome. He remembered Santiago perfectly well.

Roz had enjoyed her day. She window-shopped at famous name designer stores, she watched Madrid's beautiful people promenade along wide, tree-lined boulevards in the heart of the city, and she even took in some culture with a visit to the Prado Museum, where she gazed, awestruck, at paintings she had only ever seen on posters or in the pages of magazines.

But sightseeing is best shared, and by midafternoon, feeling a little lonely, she was back in the suite at the Santo Mauro Hotel, flicking through the TV channels, searching for something in English she could watch.

She clicked onto a channel where a documentary on bullfighting was being shown. Roz's eyes widened as a preening matador closed in for the kill on a bloodied bull, which snorted and raked the ground with one hoof as it eyed its approaching assassin. The matador raised his sword and Roz quickly pressed the remote.

She found a shopping channel. They were the same the world over: A beaming, glamorous presenter held up a thin, gold necklace as she enthusiastically told her viewers what an absolute bargain it was. Roz couldn't understand a word but she knew exactly what the presenter was saying.

Roz sighed and pressed the remote again. This time it was a cartoon channel, dubbed in Spanish. She was ready to give up when the door opened and Santiago entered carrying a bulging shopping bag.

"Were you training or shopping?" she asked him.

Santiago didn't reply. He emptied the contents of the bag onto the king-size bed. It was like Christmas had arrived early. Roz gazed at the pile of cell phones, iPods, designer sunglasses, and other assorted items that Santiago had been presented with at the end of his first day at work.

"Why do you need four phones?" asked Roz as she picked up one of the cell phones. "Can I have one?"

Santiago nodded and then opened a glossy Audi car brochure dedicated to the top-of-the-line model. "Pick a color," he said. "Any color."

Roz raised her eyebrows. "Santi, you're going to have to score a lot of goals."

6

In England, football supporters *go* to football matches. In cities and towns all over the country, they stream from every direction into the stadiums, like lines of ants returning to the nest.

At Real Madrid, the supporters *gather.* For hours before kickoff, the streets and squares around the Santiago Bernabéu Stadium gradually fill as fanatical Madridistas congregate to talk, to eat, to drink, to sing, to worship their heroes, to celebrate the spectacle they are waiting to witness.

Almost all the matches are played in the evening. As the night cools, customers spill from the bars onto the streets, souvenir and food sellers do brisk business, music pounds from mobile discos, the air is full of shouts and chants and songs, which grow louder and more passionate as kickoff approaches.

The magnificent Bernabéu towers over the city. The Bernabéu *is* football history. Its museum is one of the most visited in all of Spain. Cabinet upon cabinet line its galleries, displaying the original or the replica of the numerous trophies won by Real. From the numerous regional titles of the earliest days to the European and intercontinental trophies, they are all there, a treasure trove of honor, proudly earned and displayed for the world to see.

There are photographs and TV monitors showing grainy film of the great moments and the great players in the Real story—Di Stéfano, Puskás, Gento, and many, many more. The ghosts of the past are a constant reminder to even the *galácticos* of today of what is demanded by the club and by its supporters.

On match nights, the Bernabéu sits, like a modern-day Colosseum, and awaits the arrival of the eighty-five thousand spectators.

Slowly the heaving mass of humanity moves into the magnificent stadium and the banked tiers fill. On cold nights, massive heaters burn down from the canopy to keep off the winter chill. Floodlights turn the immaculate playing surface a dazzling emerald green. Supporters chat and chant and study the match programs as they listen for news of the team lineups and the arrival of the modern-day gladiators.

But the gladiators of ancient Rome knew nothing

of the luxury that is enjoyed by today's superstars as they prepare to enter the arena.

The dressing rooms are magnificent. Marble floors, blue and white tiled walls, individual power showers, spa baths, separate treatment areas, even the gold-finished washbasins look as though they have been specially imported from a millionaire's mansion.

In the home dressing room, each of the players' personal lockers has a huge action photograph of the superstar set into the door.

Santiago was struggling to take all this in as he sat next to Ronaldo. The chosen eleven and the substitutes were changed and ready for the coach's pre-match briefing. And although the good-natured banter was flying around the dressing room, just as it does in every dressing room before every match, there was an air of tension. Even the world's greatest players can take nothing for granted; when the whistle blows, they still have to perform.

While Santiago had been named as one of the subs, there was no guarantee that he would even get onto the field, but he was more nervous than he had ever been in his life. His cell rang and he saw that a text message had arrived.

He opened the text and read the words: *Good luck, from Julio and Grandma.*

Santiago smiled. He'd known they wouldn't forget and he knew that they would be watching the match back in L.A. on the brand-new wide-screen TV he had bought for them.

As the players around him joked and laughed, Santiago thought of his father, Herman, who for so long had been opposed to his son pursuing a career in football. They had argued fiercely many times, but unknown to Santi, when he made his debut for Newcastle, Herman had been proudly watching on a television at a bar in L.A.

Santiago learned about it much later, from his grandmother, but he never got the chance to talk about the experience with his father. Herman died from a heart attack soon after; father and son were never reconciled.

Rudi Van Der Merwe entered the dressing room and the banter immediately ceased. Van Der Merwe waited for a moment before speaking. "You only ever lose the battles you don't fight. Make me proud. Play with honor. Play with grace. And heart. But above all, play with dignity."

That was it. The talking was over. The players stood up, ready for battle to commence. In the Champions League.

7

THE CHAMPIONS LEAGUE—the world's premier club competition. For some clubs, those from the smaller footballing nations, just qualifying for the group stages is a major achievement.

The chance of home and away ties with the likes of Real Madrid, AC Milan, or Manchester United is the dream of the footballing minnows from every far-flung corner of the continent.

But for Europe's big guns, qualifying from the group stages is an absolute necessity. Tricky encounters with little-known teams who look on the matches as their own European finals are always potential banana skins waiting to be slipped on. A win is nothing more than what is expected; a defeat, and coaches and managers begin to hear the sounds of knives being sharpened.

Santiago was at the rear of the line of players making their way down the granite steps of the players' tunnel and through the blue protective covering leading to the field, but he heard the earsplitting roar of the crowd long before he stepped into the open.

Thousands of cameras flashed and the white, plastic flags that bear the Madrid logo and are freely distributed to supporters before the match were being waved in welcome, making it appear as though the Bernabéu itself was on the move.

High up in the stadium, Roz and Glen were taking their seats in one of the stunning executive boxes. There were four rows of tiered seats for the guests, and television monitors strategically placed for close-up views of the action.

Roz noticed the inquisitive and slightly critical looks cast in her direction by a couple of expensively dressed young women who were presumably the wives or girlfriends of other players. But Roz was too nervous for Santiago to worry, for the moment, about how she measured up.

She turned to Glen. "Santi'll be bricking it by now."

Glen nodded. "He's not the only one."

In L.A., Santiago's grandmother, Mercedes, a long-time fan of Real Madrid who was as knowledgeable as anyone on the fine points of football, had invited the neighbors in to watch the match. And not just the next-door neighbors; half the neighborhood was crammed into the tiny living room of the house, which sat on a hillside, almost in the shadow of Dodger Stadium.

Mercedes and Julio had invited all their friends, and had made sure they had the best seats in the house.

A graphic showing the teams and subs appeared on the TV, and Julio yelled in delight as he saw the final name in the Real list. "Look, Grandma. Santiago is one of the subs!"

Mercedes nodded but said nothing; she was only happy when her grandson was *on* the field.

In the stadium, Santiago was making his way to the substitutes' bench. Before he took his seat he glanced up to the bank of seats reserved for club officials and VIPs. There was even a seat that was always reserved for the king of Spain.

Santiago's eyes settled on the club president, Señor Pérez, and on Burruchaga, the director of football. Everyone was expecting so much from him, if he got his chance.

Away to the left, the infamous group of supporters known as the *Ultras Sur* were well into their familiar chants, drums were beating, and white flags and scarves were urging the referee to get the match under way.

And then it was. Real was facing Olympiakos of Greece in their first match and from the outset the Madrid team slipped into its silky, stylish rhythm.

Zidane beguiled the opposition with a series of deft touches, Beckham supplied an array of raking, cross-field passes, Ronaldo made bustling, probing runs, and Gavin Harris, who hadn't scored for fourteen matches, was unfortunate with a couple of half chances.

Santiago watched every moment, marveling at the many flashes of brilliance. But for all the dazzling skills, there were no goals in the first half, and the teams left the field to regroup and reconsider tactics.

In the dressing room, Santiago sat with the others, listening intently as the coach talked of subtle changes in tactics and urged his players on to greater effort.

The minutes passed swiftly and soon Santi was back on the bench as the second half settled into a similar pattern to the first. Near misses, moments of magic, half chances.

The clock ticked around to the eightieth minute and the sense of frustration was as acute for the Madrid players as it was for their supporters.

Van Der Merwe looked along the bench and gestured for Santiago to warm up.

Santi felt his heart begin to pound. As he got to his feet he realized that he could hardly stand up, let alone warm up. He forced himself to move and began to jog toward the *Ultras Sur,* keeping his eyes on the action.

From a ball out wide, Gavin Harris had a glorious opportunity to snatch a goal. But with only the keeper to beat from five yards out, he pushed his shot wide of an upright.

The crowd bayed its displeasure and as Santi jogged back toward the bench, the nod from his coach was all that was necessary to tell him to get ready to go on. He stripped off his tracksuit, feeling, almost hearing, his heart thudding in his chest.

Gavin was the man to make way for Santiago. As they met on the touchline, he embraced his friend and Santi ran to take up his position, to the welcoming roars of the Bernabéu.

There was no more time for nerves; he had to make his mark.

Up in the executive box and out in L.A., Santiago's loved ones were praying that the few remaining minutes of the match would be enough for him to at least give a glimpse of his skills.

But at first, nothing happened for him. He made a couple of runs, but the other members of the team were not yet familiar with his style of play.

He was close to the halfway line when he heard his coach shout his name.

Santiago looked over to Van Der Merwe and saw him gesturing for him to drop into the space on the left, just outside the box. Santi nodded and jogged into position.

Real pressed again, desperately searching for a late win, and from a deflected shot from Ronaldo, they won a corner.

David Beckham hurried to the corner flag and curved in a great ball, but an Olympiakos defender just managed to jump his highest to head it away from the danger area.

Santiago was lurking at the edge of the box. He watched the ball as it dropped toward him. There wasn't time to think about passes, or to look for teammates in better positions; the ball was just asking—crying out—for a first-time volley.

Which was exactly what it got.

Santiago timed his shot perfectly and the ball hurtled at ferocious speed across the box and into the top corner of the net.

The entire stadium seemed to erupt. On the touchline Van Der Merwe, Steve McManaman, Gavin Harris, and the other Madrid substitutes leaped to their feet and punched the air in triumph. Up in their executive box Glen and Roz were hugging each other as the other guests watched. In L.A. the screams of joy were echoing down the street. And on the field Santiago was engulfed by his fellow Madrid players.

When he finally emerged from the scrum, he looked up to the heavens and silently dedicated his goal to his father.

The last few minutes passed agonizingly slowly for Real as Olympiakos pressed for an equalizer, but then the referee's whistle sounded for the last time and Santiago heard his name ringing around the Bernabéu.

8

Rosa-Maria found it difficult to hide her emotions as she watched Santiago's postmatch interview on the TV in the bar.

The regulars were following the interview closely, nodding sagely as Santiago attempted to describe his feelings at the moment he saw the ball crash into the net.

Young Enrique was standing at the back of the bar, watching the watchers. When he was certain that everyone else was focused on the TV, he struck.

A wallet was invitingly perched on one of the tables, temporarily ignored by its owner. Swiftly and skillfully, Enrique snatched it away and then slipped quickly through the rear door of the bar.

Only one person saw what had happened.

Out in the dark alley behind the bar, an older teenager called Tito was waiting for Enrique. He held out his hands as the younger boy approached and snatched the wallet away, pulling out the few notes and then checking to see if there were any credit cards.

Before either of them could speak, the back door of the bar swung open again. The older boy glared at his young partner in crime, threw the wallet to the ground, and then turned and ran with the cash.

Enrique had no time to follow. Before he could move he was roughly grabbed. He winced as he heard his mother's furious voice. "Have you lost your mind?"

The teenager tried to struggle free but there was no escaping. Rosa held him firmly by the shoulders, her eyes ablaze. "You want me to visit you in jail? You make the wrong choice now and there's no going back."

Enrique stopped struggling and just stared at the ground as his mother spoke more calmly, trying to make him see sense. "Enrique, don't you realize this is wrong?"

"Like I have choices," snapped Enrique.

"But of course you do. That new Real player, Muñez, he had nothing, just like you. And look at him now."

"Yeah, look at him now," sneered Enrique. "He

was poor and I'm gonna *stay* poor. We got so much in common, right?"

He wrenched himself free and went to walk away.

"Enrique, wait!" shouted Rosa-Maria.

The teenager stopped and looked back. His mother was staring at him, but her eyes were suddenly fearful and uncertain.

"What?" said Enrique. "What is it?"

Rosa-Maria glanced at the door to the bar, as if she were afraid that someone might come out and overhear what she was about to say. "Enrique, you must promise not to tell your father," she said, almost in a whisper. "But I have a secret that I left in Mexico."

Paparazzi. A word common to every language; the gangs of freelance photographers are known the world over. They lurk outside nightclubs and fashionable restaurants, they haunt the homes of the superstars, they wait on beaches, outside hotels, and at airports in the hope of snatching a one-off picture that will earn them big money from the tabloid newspapers or glossy magazines.

Sometimes they hunt in packs; on other occasions they operate singly, but the aim is always the same: Snatch a celebrity photo that will sell, the more compromising or embarrassing for the victim the better.

The paparazzi were out in force as Gavin, Santi, Glen, and Roz stepped from the vehicle outside one of Madrid's most fashionable restaurants. Cameras flashed as their owners jostled for position and shouted for attention.

Roz stayed close to Santiago, blinking at the flashes and the unwanted, intimidating attention.

A voice nearby shouted out in English, "Oi, darling, show us a bit of leg!"

Roz turned angrily in the direction of the voice and as she did, one of her heels caught on the pavement. She tripped and stumbled forward, falling to the ground. It was a perfect paparazzi moment; the night was flooded with white light and the synchronized sound of clicking cameras.

Santi and Glen rushed to help Roz to her feet while Gavin stood back and smiled for the photographers, making sure they got him from his best angle.

Roz was still shaken as they made their way into the restaurant, where a beaming maître d' was waiting for them. Gavin reached into a jacket pocket and handed over some notes to the maître d', who smiled and gestured for them to follow.

He wasn't leading them to a table. They went straight through the restaurant into the kitchens, past cooks and waiters, who nodded their thanks as Gavin handed out more euros, and then out through a door at the back into a narrow, dimly lit passageway.

On the other side was the entrance to another restaurant, smaller, a lot more discreet, and totally paparazzi-free. Gavin ushered them in and the restaurant owner welcomed him like an old friend.

The atmosphere was much quieter and a lot more relaxed, but before they could finally enjoy their meal in peace, they had to endure one more photo as the owner added to his collection of pictures of the rich and famous visitors to his establishment.

Glen turned to Gavin. "Is it like this all the time?"

"It is, actually," answered Gavin. "They're all mad. Total lunatics."

"You love it though, don't you?" said Roz as she tried to fix the broken heel of her shoe. "All this attention."

"At the end of the day, I'd much rather be out with my friends," said Gavin with a shrug. "Having a nice meal, with some good conversation. There's more to life than just football."

Roz thought back to the time when Gavin and Santiago had shared an apartment in Newcastle. She smiled. "What, you mean like Xbox games?"

Gavin grinned. "Don't get me wrong, I do love it and it pays the bills. But I've got other interests now."

He reached for a bottle of red wine and poured some into a glass for Roz. "Like this."

"Like what?" said Roz as Gavin poured wine for the others.

"Wine. I've made an investment in a tasty little vineyard in France. Could be my future."

Roz lifted the glass to her mouth and took a sip. She swallowed the wine and then screwed up her nose and grimaced. "It's spoiled!"

Gavin's eyes widened. "Is it?" He grabbed the bottle, took a sniff at the wine, and shrugged as if to say, *Smells all right to me.* He was checking the label when a couple of familiar figures approached. One was Barry Rankin, Gavin's agent, and the other was the Real Madrid and former Everton midfielder, Thomas Gravesen.

Gravesen nodded a hello and headed for their table, but Rankin stopped. "How's the fettuccini?" He saw the bottle in Gavin's hand. "Try the '95, Gavin, it's got a lovely nose on it."

"You know everyone, right?" said Gavin, wisely deciding that maybe it wasn't the moment to demonstrate any more of his newly found expertise as a wine connoisseur.

Rankin nodded. Before Santiago had signed up with Glen, Rankin had made a couple of attempts to get in first. He reached for Roz's right hand and kissed it. "Charmed."

Roz snatched her hand back as Rankin turned to Glen. "Mr. Foy, lovely to see you."

"Barry," said Glen, looking as though the feeling was far from mutual.

But disdainful looks and rejection meant nothing to Barry Rankin; it was all part of the job as far as he was concerned. He reached across the table to shake Santiago's hand. "Let's do coffee sometime, Santi."

He smiled once more and then continued to his table as Roz looked at the hand he had kissed. "I hope I didn't catch anything," she said.

Glen and Roz were booked on an early flight back to England the following morning; there was just enough time for Santiago to go with them to the airport before being driven to training.

The car journey passed in virtual silence. Glen was in the front with the driver and Roz and Santi were in the back, neither of them looking forward to the moment of parting.

They reached the airport and as Glen tactfully hovered a couple of feet away and the driver stood waiting with a rear door open, Santi and Roz hugged and then kissed good-bye.

"Come on," said Roz quietly to Santiago. "Jump on the plane with us. No one will know."

Santiago smiled. "I think my new coach might notice."

"But the house is so empty without you, Santi."

"You'll be fine. It's only a couple of weeks. It'll be like you never left."

"I love you," said Roz, not caring if Glen, or the driver, or the whole world, heard her words.

Santi was a little more reserved. "Me, too."

They kissed again and then Roz wrapped her arms around Santiago, reluctant to let him go. As Santi looked over Roz's shoulder, he saw the driver tap his watch and gesture that it was time to leave.

Glen had seen it, too. "Right, then," he said loudly, "time to go, Roz. We'll miss the plane."

Roz sighed and picked up her suitcase and Glen went to Santiago and shook his hand firmly. "Call me if you need me, son."

And then they were gone, and Santiago was heading toward the training ground, suddenly feeling very alone.

9

THE DAYS PASSED SWIFTLY and Santiago quickly settled into the new training routine and found himself more at ease with his new teammates. He continued to marvel at the skills of not only the *galácticos* but also of the new younger generation of Real players like Robinho and Sergio Ramos.

And the other members of the squad recognized that Santiago had the talent, pace, and instinctive, predatory touch of a natural goal scorer to become a worthy wearer of the famous white shirt of Real.

Santiago loved scoring goals in practice matches almost as much as in the real thing. From the sitter to the spectacular, each one gave him a buzz, but especially the spectacular, which had become something of a Muñez trademark. And that could only be a good thing at Real Madrid, where the fans had been brought up on the spectacular.

The Real coach, Rudi Van Der Merwe, was not the flamboyant type. He went about his business in his own particular way. He was totally effective and thorough, a motivator. He had his players' respect and no one messed with him.

And Van Der Merwe never seemed to miss a thing. During training he seemed to have the ability to talk on his cell phone, check lists of stats or notes prepared by his assistants, and still be aware of everything that was going on around him.

He was talking on his cell when his eyes settled on Gavin Harris, over sixty feet away on the field.

Van Der Merwe finished the phone conversation and then beckoned to his chief physical therapist. "Harris's calcaneus deltoid is playing up," he said as soon as the physio joined him. "Keep an eye on it."

The physio stared at his boss and then turned to watch Gavin as he ran for a ball. Only a highly trained and skilled eye would have noticed the slight hesitation in stride. The physio turned back to Van Der Merwe and nodded.

On the training field Santiago had just scored with a shot from barely inside the box when Van Der

Merwe spotted the club's director of football, Señor Burruchaga, walking toward him.

Burruchaga had made no secret of his admiration for Real's new signing and had already hinted that he believed Santiago should be in the starting lineup.

Both the coach and the director of football were fully aware of their responsibilities at Real. The coaching and team selection were up to Van Der Merwe, while other footballing matters, such as identifying and pursuing transfer targets, were Burruchaga's domain. It was the common European system, and one increasingly adopted by British clubs.

But Burruchaga didn't always appreciate where his job ended and Van Der Merwe's began. He joined Van Der Merwe on the touchline and glanced over at Santiago as he jogged back toward the center circle.

"You think Muñez is ready for a full game?" said Burruchaga without looking at Van Der Merwe.

The coach shook his head. "No. Not yet. I think he needs to settle for a while."

But Burruchaga obviously had different ideas. He turned and looked deliberately at the coach. "Maybe you should think again."

He walked away, giving Van Der Merwe no chance to reply.

There were always young fans hanging around the training ground entrance as the players made their way to and from the complex. They clustered around their heroes in the hope of a word or an autograph.

Santiago always had time for the fans. He knew where they were coming from, particularly the obviously poorer kids. He'd been there for most of his life, and now that life was so much better he didn't forget. So when a group of youngsters came hurtling toward him as he left training that day he stopped and took the pens, photographs, programs, and scraps of paper that were thrust toward him.

He thought he had signed for them all before heading to his car, but at the back of the noisy gaggle of youngsters, one smaller kid stood clutching a ball he had wanted autographed.

It was Enrique and he had missed his chance. He turned away looking hugely disappointed and began the long walk home.

He was deep in thought as he wandered down the central divide of one of the highways that ring the city. Vehicles hurtled by in both directions, but Enrique seemed oblivious to the roar of engines and the hot blasts of air as huge trucks thundered past just a few feet away.

After negotiations with the club management . . .

Santi signs for Real Madrid.

Santi trains hard alongside
his old friend Gavin.

And as Gavin loses his touch . . .

. . . Santi begins to make his mark.

It's a new life for Santi: new car, new people for him and Roz to meet . . .

. . . but an old joke!

There's plenty of interest from the press . . .

. . . and the fans.

As Santi
comes on
again to
score . . .

. . . Gavin
reads of
their rivalry
in the press.

Enrique dreams of
meeting his hero.

He reached a dusty expanse of waste ground and meandered toward the outskirts of the city. When he arrived at the metro he did what he always did: He jumped over the turnstile. Enrique didn't think about paying for the ride, and anyway, he couldn't, because he had no cash.

Eventually he came to the all-too-familiar surroundings of his home. The aging, crumbling blocks of apartments, the narrow, neglected streets. This was the other side of Madrid, the side that Roz had not even glimpsed during her day of sightseeing.

Enrique walked along a narrow back alley and emerged to see a gang of his friends playing football on a bone-dry scrap of land. It wasn't the Bernabéu, but for the kids tearing from one end to another as they battled and shouted for the ball, it could have been.

Enrique dropped his own ball and rushed to join them and soon he was in the thick of the action. He took a pass from one of his friends and skipped away, easily avoiding a couple of clumsy tackles as the dust swirled around him.

He lifted his head and prepared to shoot for goal, through the couple of ragged sweatshirts dumped on the ground that represented goalposts.

Before the youngster could bring his foot through

10

REAL'S EARLY SEASON form was good, but it could
have been better. The team was beginning to gel in
most areas, from defense through to attack, with one
notable and very obvious exception—Gavin Harris.

Coach Van Der Merwe was giving his misfiring
striker every opportunity to rediscover his shooting
boots but it was proving a painful process.

Santiago was becoming accustomed to spending
each match on the bench, with only brief cameo appearances to his name. He knew he had been impress-
ing in training, but Van Der Merwe seemed set on
making his newest signing wait for a full ninety-
minute appearance.

It was difficult for both Santi and Gavin. They
were the best of friends, but they were professionals

and they knew that they were rivals for the one coveted place in the starting lineup.

Santi got his chance to show the boss exactly what he could offer in a La Liga game. He was occupying his usual seat on the bench, watching with growing frustration as his teammates battled to overcome stubborn and determined opposition.

Gavin was trying his heart out but he was always slightly off the pace, which didn't help when he botched the best chance of the game from close in.

The crowd groaned as one and Gavin shook his head and turned away from the goal, avoiding making eye contact with his teammates.

On the bench, Van Der Merwe turned to Santiago and gestured for him to go on. Gavin's number was already being held up on the substitution board. He was coming off.

He met Santiago on the touchline and smiled as they touched hands. Santi ran on, kissing his necklace for luck, but Gavin's smile turned to a scowl as he went to the bench, glaring at the coach.

"I could've gone the whole game, boss," he said, taking his seat alongside the subs.

Van Der Merwe was watching Santiago run toward the penalty box. He didn't look at Gavin as he replied, "We need young blood, Harris."

There were not many minutes left; Santiago, once again, had little time to try to find the rhythm and pace of the game.

Roz was sitting alone up in the stands. She was wearing a Real scarf, gripping it tightly, willing Santiago to make another telling contribution to the match.

An opposing player went down after a tackle and rolled on the turf in apparent agony. The challenge had looked innocuous enough, and the Madridistas whistled their displeasure at the apparent time-wasting tactics as the ref allowed the player to receive treatment.

Sometimes a sudden change of personnel in the opposition can unsettle and temporarily confuse even the most experienced of defenders. And that was exactly what happened.

Soon after the restart, the Real keeper, Casillas, gathered the ball and threw it out to Salgado. He moved swiftly away on the right flank before passing to Guti, who played the ball quickly to Raúl, who instantly back-heeled it to Beckham and then ran to collect a clever one-two.

The opposing defenders were being dragged out of position as they tried to figure out and counter Santi's pace and positioning.

They didn't have time. After a jinking run from Ronaldo, and a swift interchange of passes between

Guti and Graven, the ball went out to Beckham on the right. He sent a looping cross into the box and from close to the penalty spot, Santiago leapt into the air and executed a spectacular scissors kick, which beat the keeper low down to his left.

Santiago had come off the bench again to grab a winner close to the end, and as the cheers rang around the Bernabéu, every one of his Real teammates rushed to congratulate the super sub.

Gavin was facedown on a physical therapist's bed, receiving treatment after the match. His thigh was hurting badly, even though the physio was an expert at his job, applying exactly the right amount of pressure in exactly the right places.

Gavin grimaced, trying to hide the pain, as Santiago entered the treatment room, already showered and dressed and doing his best not to show too much delight at scoring the winning goal.

"Hey, come on, Gavin," he called. "How much longer are you gonna lay there?"

His friend turned and smiled. "I can't turn down a free Swedish massage, can I? Pedro here is very sensitive. I wouldn't want to hurt his feelings."

The physio had heard it all before. He just smiled and gave the player a slap on the thigh.

As Gavin feigned mock agony he saw Van Der Merwe walk into the room. He sat up quickly and grinned at the coach, not wanting him to think that there was anything seriously amiss. "All right, boss?"

"How's the thigh?" asked Van Der Merwe.

"Good as new, boss."

Van Der Merwe was not easily convinced; he could see straight through Gavin's bravado. "The human body is a biological wonder. It can achieve miracles, but it is not indestructible." He was staring straight into Gavin's eyes. "Football. The running, the falls, the tackles. We all have a shelf life. Remember that."

For once, Gavin seemed lost for words, but Santiago was ready to leap to his friend's defense. He looked at Van Der Merwe. "Even you, boss?"

Gavin's eyes flicked from Santiago to Van Der Merwe. He was expecting some sort of reprimand, but the coach just smiled, silently appreciating Santiago's fighting spirit.

For a few moments no one said a word until Santiago decided that perhaps he had gone a little too far with the few words he had directed at his new boss. He knew how much playing football meant to Gavin, despite all his talk about new business ventures and vineyards. Surely Van Der Merwe could understand that.

Santiago looked at the coach. "Don't you miss playing?"

Van Der Merwe considered for a moment before replying. "A lot of people would give anything in the world to be in your position, Muñez. I'm not one of them."

He turned and started to leave as Gavin eased himself from the treatment table. "Hey, boss?" he called.

Van Der Merwe stopped by the doorway and looked back.

Gavin was back to his usual, irrepressible self. "Aren't you gonna wish me a happy birthday?"

11

GAVIN WAS FAMOUS not just for his football, but also for his parties, and he had decided that this birthday bash was going to be one of his most memorable.

As Santiago and Roz walked into Gavin's rented villa in the hills above Madrid their eyes widened in disbelief. The place must have been worth a fortune, and not a small fortune.

It sprawled over a huge area on different levels. The main room was like the most exclusive nightclub in the world, with designer furniture and modern artwork that looked as if had been loaned by one of Madrid's major galleries. Through sliding smoked glass doors, they glimpsed an indoor pool lit as dramatically as the rest of the house.

Music was thumping and everywhere there were

people. Most of the team had been invited. They were mingling with Madrid's beautiful people, smiling, laughing, chatting. There appeared to be at least three girls to every guy. But that wasn't a surprise; it was Gavin's party.

Santi was beginning to feel part of it all. He was wearing a perfectly cut black suit and feeling as cool as he looked. As Santi and Roz edged their way through the room, looking for Gavin, everyone was smiling or nodding their appreciation and admiration for the new kid on the block, the new goal-scoring sensation.

Gavin appeared, squeezing his way through a clutch of beautiful women. He grabbed a bottle of champagne and some glasses from a passing waitress and beamed at Santiago and Roz. "Welcome to the Pleasuredome!"

"Happy birthday, Gavin," said Roz, kissing him on the cheek. "Twenty-nine again?"

Gavin just grinned. "So what do you think of all this? Leased it from some friend of Madonna's."

"Yeah, it's beautiful," said Roz. "But does the Pleasuredome have a loo? I'm desperate."

The birthday boy pointed across the room and Roz headed off while Santiago took the glass of champagne Gavin pressed into his hand.

Santi was still gazing in awe around the luxurious villa. "This must have set you back a few bucks."

Gavin shrugged. "Barry sorts it all out. I just sit back and enjoy the ride."

As if on cue, Barry Rankin came wandering over, a fat cigar held between two fingers of his right hand and each arm wrapped around a beautiful girl. "All right, my son," he said, as the girls detached themselves and planted birthday kisses on Gavin's cheeks.

Rankin obviously enjoyed having his arms around someone, so he draped one across Santi's shoulders and pulled him close. "Santi—cracking goal tonight. Respect. But what are you thinking bringing Roz here, man? This is what you could call a *singles* party, *amigo.*"

He guided Santi across the crowded room and out through the rear doors. On a five-a-side field a couple of Madrid players were showing off their skills to a group of girls and close to the house, more bikini-clad girls were posing, rather than swimming, in the outdoor pool.

Rankin looked at the girls and then at Santiago and raised his eyebrows.

"Roz is my fiancée," said Santiago.

"Yeah," said Rankin as he stared at the girls in the pool. "And soon she'll be back in Newcastle defrosting her ravioli meal-for-one while you're out here surrounded by . . ." He looked at the girls in the pool again. ". . . all this. Think I fancy a swim."

Rankin strolled away and Santiago went back into the villa to find Roz. He found Gavin first and they were speaking together when a tall, glamorous woman with long, gleaming, dark hair and a smile that could have graced a toothpaste ad eased her way up to them.

"Good evening, Gavin," she said in excellent English. "Aren't you going to introduce me to your friend?"

"Of course," answered Gavin, suddenly not quite his usual, brash self. "Jordana García, meet Santiago Muñez."

As Jordana fixed her eyes on Santiago, Gavin reached up and gently stroked her cheek. "She can't resist me."

Jordana didn't look away from Santiago. "I'll try." She offered her right hand to Santiago and they shook.

"*Hola*, Santiago."

"*Hola*."

"Nice suit. Dolce?"

Santiago nodded.

"Not a bad goal tonight. You must be exhausted after, what was it, seven whole minutes on the pitch."

She was still holding his hand.

"Hands off, Jordana," said Gavin. "He's spoken for."

Jordana released Santi's hand and then glanced at Gavin with a look that said, *So what?* She smiled at Santi again.

Roz was battling her way through the partying hordes, feeling completely out of place. There were so many tanned, beautiful women around, every one of them with the looks and figure of a supermodel. It was all a long way from Newcastle.

Finally, she found Santi at the bar with the most glamorous, sophisticated-looking woman of the lot.

"Roz," said Santi quickly. "This is Jordana. She's in television over here."

The two women smiled, sizing each other up.

"Hi," said Jordana. "Santi was just telling me about your wedding plans. You're a lucky woman."

"Not half as lucky as he is," countered Roz.

Jordana turned back to Santiago and spoke in Spanish. "I'll have to get you on my show sometime, before every station in Europe snaps you up."

Santiago could see Roz's irritation at being excluded from the conversation. He pointedly replied in English, "Thanks, but I'm not into all that stuff."

Roz's look of irritation was turning to one of anger. She'd understood nothing of Jordana's comment and Santiago's reply left her wondering exactly what the television presenter had suggested.

And it didn't get any better as Jordana raised her eyebrows with a look of mock shock and said to Santi, "Excuse me, but did you just say no to me?"

Santi laughed and so did Jordana. But Roz just smiled politely. She didn't get the joke, and she didn't want to.

It was a long, long night, even by Madrid standards; almost time to get up by the time Santi and Roz prepared for bed back at their suite at the hotel.

Roz had been burning to ask Santi a question ever since her encounter with Jordana, and she couldn't wait any longer. "What did you think of that TV woman?"

"Who?" answered Santiago innocently.

"You know exactly who I mean. Miss 'Did you just say no to me?' Did you like her?"

Santiago shrugged. "She's okay. I think Gavin has a thing for her."

"Well, she definitely likes you."

Roz was watching Santi closely, waiting to see how he responded, and Santi could sense his fiancée's feeling of insecurity. But instead of being instantly reassuring he decided to tease her a little. "Well, I am pretty irresistible."

"Yeah, and bigheaded, too," snapped Roz.

Santiago laughed as he grabbed Roz and pulled her close. He kissed her gently and then looked into her eyes. "I love *you*, Roz. Remember?"

12

THE CAR DREW UP OUTSIDE an imposing, futuristic-looking mansion with huge windows and towering, square columns supporting the massive roof.

Roz stared from the car window. "Santi, why are we here?"

Santiago was already out of the vehicle. As Roz followed, gazing up at the impressive but imposing façade, he gestured proudly. "This is our house."

Roz's eyes widened. "You've . . . you've bought it?"

Santiago nodded enthusiastically. "Yeah, I did."

"Oh. Oh, you haven't?"

"Yeah. What do you think?"

Before Roz could answer, Santiago, with a smile that was almost as wide as the mansion, was dragging her toward the front door. "Wait 'til you see inside."

The interior was just as impressive and just as

overwhelming. Roz followed Santiago around, almost in a daze. Huge rooms, some on split levels, most of them painted a dazzling white. Enormous canvases of bewildering modern art, cascades of flowers in massive glass vases. So much, almost too much, to take in.

"This is nice," said Roz as she followed Santi into the state-of-the-art kitchen.

Santi pulled a bottle of champagne from a fridge big enough to hold a side of beef. "I wanted to surprise you; I knew you'd love it. It belonged to some very famous designer. It's got seven bedrooms, each with en suite bathrooms."

He was starting to sound like a real estate agent. Roz wandered back into the main living room as Santiago wrestled with the cork on the champagne bottle.

The place *was* beautiful, but in a cold, almost clinical way, and to Roz, at least, it didn't feel like a home.

She stood gazing up at an ugly modern painting, trying to work out what it meant, or even if it had been hung the right way, as Santiago came in with two glasses of foaming champagne.

"A lot of the decorations inside the house and the furniture were designed by the guy who owned it." He looked around at their new home. "Do you like it?"

"Er . . . I don't know what to say," said Roz as she took the glass Santiago offered. He hadn't picked up the irony in her voice; he was buzzing with excitement and almost exploding with pride.

Roz lifted her glass and joined Santi in the toast to their new home, trying desperately to like it as much as he did.

Santi took one quick sip of the champagne and then checked his watch. "I have to go. See you after training. There's a set of keys for you in the kitchen, so make yourself . . . at home." He kissed her quickly and then hurried away. Roz sighed and sipped her champagne. She looked up at the modern painting again and decided that, whatever it was meant to be, it was watching her. And she didn't like it.

The place was so quiet, more like a museum than a house. Roz went upstairs to take a closer look at the *Palacio de Muñez*. In the master bedroom she switched on the TV before continuing with her tour. The sound of other voices was comforting, even television voices speaking in Spanish.

When Roz had checked out the six other bedrooms with their six en suite bathrooms, she found her way back by following the sound of the television voices. A daytime magazine program was in full swing but Roz didn't even glance at the screen as she went to look at the largest and most lavish en suite bathroom of the lot.

It was only as she emerged and heard the name Santiago Muñez that she looked at the TV. Two presenters were discussing the previous night's match and Roz glared as she realized that one of the presenters was . . . Jordana.

Roz picked up the TV remote and stabbed violently at the OFF button.

It was another brief visit. Roz had juggled her shifts with other nurses to make the trip possible, and on the day before her return to Newcastle, she left the new house in an attempt to make herself more familiar with Madrid.

She wasn't adapting very well to this new way of living. It was fine for Santi; he had his football, his friends, his teammates. Roz had only Santiago. Her work, her friends, everything she knew and liked was in another country.

But she left the house determined to find her way around and learn more about the city. Two hours later she was lost in a run-down district far from the usual tourist attractions and feeling slightly scared by some of the hostile looks she was getting from the locals.

She was relieved when her cell phone rang. It was her mom, Carol, calling from a hairdressing salon back in Newcastle.

Carol loved the fame by association she was getting these days and after a quick hello she made sure all the other clients at the hairdressers' knew exactly what she was talking about. "I'm reading a magazine, pet. It's full of pictures of Gavin's party. There's one of you and Santi opposite a pic of the Beckhams. Did you get talking to Victoria?"

"No, Mum."

"Oh, really?" said Carol, making it sound as if Roz and Victoria were the best of friends. "Her David's looking fine. Are those new shoes you're wearing?"

"Yes, Mum."

"They go lovely with that handbag."

"Thanks, Mum."

In the salon, Carol was studying all the photographs closely. She spoke more quietly. "One thing, Roz, love."

"Yes, Mum?"

"You could do with a bit of spray tan, pet."

When she ended the call, Roz was feeling even more depressed. She headed back toward the city center and came to a busy road where she had to wait to cross at the traffic lights.

As she turned to look in the direction of the oncoming traffic, a moped flashed by and the young rider quickly reached out and snatched Roz's handbag, almost knocking her to the ground.

Before she could even shout, the moped had disappeared. Roz turned and looked at the other pedestrians waiting to cross. No one said a word.

Santiago was watching television. Bored. He'd had a good day at training, Van Der Merwe had praised his commitment and work ethic, and he'd arrived home both feeling good and that soon he'd get his chance in the starting lineup.

As he drew up in the Audi, he'd seen Roz sitting outside the locked house, unable to get in because her keys had been in the stolen handbag.

Since then, they'd spent a difficult few hours and now Roz was sitting at the long dining table, surrounded by medical textbooks and files full of notes as she studied for her exams, which were approaching fast.

Santi flicked off the TV and walked over to Roz, still with the remote in one hand. He stood behind her and rested the remote on the table, looking down at the vivid photographs in the textbooks of infected wounds and open sores.

He grimaced—they weren't exactly the sort of pictures to encourage a romantic evening—but he leaned forward and kissed Roz's neck.

Roz continued with her notes. "I've got to study,

Santi. This is my chance to do some specialist, surgical nursing. I don't want to stay on the wards forever."

Santiago reached over to the book and closed it. "You can study on the plane tomorrow."

"I need to do it now," said Roz, opening the book again. "And I'm tired."

"Yeah, me, too," said Santi. "But I'm not gonna see you for another two weeks."

Roz took a deep breath, picked up the TV remote from the table, and pressed the ON button. She looked up at Santiago and handed him the remote.

Roz worked until late; her trips to Madrid were causing her to fall behind on the work she had to do for her exams. When she woke up the following morning, she turned over in bed to see that Santiago was not there.

She pulled on a dressing gown and went down to the kitchen to get some orange juice from the fridge.

On the fridge door was a note, held in place by a Real Madrid logo magnet.

The note read:

Gone to training. A driver will pick you up at noon. Have a safe flight, will call you later. S xx

Roz sighed and pulled open the fridge door.

13

AT REAL MADRID everything is based on meticulous preparation. Even when they are playing at the Bernabéu, the squad gathers at a luxury hotel in the city on the evening before the match and spends the night there.

The following day is devoted to a gradual buildup to the match. Light meals, tactical discussion with the coaching team, and plenty of relaxation before the entire squad is ferried by bus the short distance to the Bernabéu for the match itself.

It's similar to how an English team might approach an FA Cup final. The difference is that Real does it for every game.

Santiago was relaxing in the Jacuzzi in the hotel spa with his teammates Casillas, Gravesen, and Guti. Gavin had just climbed from the pool and slipped into a white terry-cloth robe.

As the others chatted and joked, he reached into his robe pocket and pulled out one of his cell phones. He punched in a number and the call was answered quickly.

"Hello?"

"Hey, Jordana. You busy?"

The television presenter instantly recognized the English accent. "Gavin. You know I always have time for you."

Gavin glanced back at the players lounging in the Jacuzzi. "I'm going crazy in here. It's like a five-star prison full of blokes. D'you fancy joining me? It's a shame to waste such a nice cell."

Jordana laughed. "I'd love to, Gavin, but I have no time. And you should rest. You need to score tonight."

This time Gavin laughed. "That's why I phoned you."

Jordana's put-down was razor sharp. "Gavin, darling, scoring *off* the pitch is not your problem."

Gavin winced; he'd walked into that and he was aware as everyone that he desperately needed to get a goal or two—and soon.

Someone in the Jacuzzi cracked a joke and the others hooted with laughter.

"Is Muñez with you?" said Jordana.

"Yeah."

"Put him on."

Jordana certainly had some nerve; Gavin almost laughed at the cheek of it. He looked over at Santi and held up the phone. "Someone wants a word."

Gavin threw the phone, taking Santi by surprise. He grabbed at it and missed and the phone was only inches from the bubbling Jacuzzi when Casillas's lightning reflexes saved it from a watery end.

The Spanish goalkeeper put the phone to his ear and adopted the worst American accent any of them had heard as he spoke. "Hey, baby, Santi here. What's happenin', sugar?"

The others thought it was hilarious and even Gavin smiled, but Santiago snatched the cell away. "Hello?"

"Hi, Santi, it's Jordana, from Gavin's party."

Santiago was hardly likely to have forgotten their first encounter. "Yeah, hi."

"My producers are very keen to get you on the show. I told them you'd do it as a favor. I knew you wouldn't mind."

The other players were watching and listening intently, as interested as Jordana was in Santiago's reply.

By the time they climbed from the Jacuzzi, Santi had suffered ten minutes of good-natured ribbing. They went to the showers where Ronaldo was already standing beneath a stream of hot water. The brilliant

Brazilian listened with a smile as the phone-call story was recounted once again.

Gavin, Santi, and Gravesen, wearing just towels around their waists and hotel slippers on their feet, got into the elevator together to return to their rooms.

Santiago didn't notice the look that Gavin and Gravesen exchanged as Gavin pressed the elevator button.

The elevator moved and then stopped with the familiar ping as the doors slid open. Santiago's eyes widened; they'd stopped at the hotel lobby.

The next second he felt the towel around his waist being yanked away and both Gavin and Gravesen shoved him out of the elevator as Gavin hit the button again.

The doors were almost closed as Santiago looked back and saw his grinning teammates waving at him.

"Adios, amigo!" Gavin exclaimed with a smile just before the doors met and the elevator began to rise.

The hotel lobby came to a standstill as receptionists and guests stared at the stark naked young man desperately trying to hide his embarrassment with one hand at the front and one at the back. He wanted to run but there was nowhere to run to; he wanted to hide but there was nowhere to hide; so he just stood there, frozen like a statue with a manic grin on his face.

It got even worse when the Real coach, Van Der

Merwe, entered the lobby from the street. He saw Santiago instantly—he could hardly miss him—and he walked straight up to the young player.

Van Der Merwe had seen the old "shove him naked out of the elevator" gag played many times before. "Looks like you forgot something, Muñez."

Santiago swallowed hard. "Yes, boss." He was desperate to cover his embarrassment as he began punching at the elevator buttons.

The coach watched him, completely straight-faced. "And, Muñez?"

"Yes, boss?"

"What is it I tell you that matters most?"

Santiago thought for a moment before replying. "Dignity, boss. Dignity."

Van Der Merwe nodded and then walked away. Santiago didn't see the slight smile on his face.

Every striker goes through spells when the goals just won't come. A lean period, a drought. It happens to the very best and when it does all the player can do is keep his head down and keep going.

But sometimes even that doesn't work. A striker's game is based on instinct, on naturally sensing the moment to make the run, to hit the shot, to leap for the header. When everything goes well it can almost be easy, or, at least, it can look easy to the supporters.

But when it goes wrong, when the goals dry up, when the striker has to *try* too hard, then it can be embarrassingly painful to watch, and the star front man suddenly looks like an awkward novice.

Managers and teammates try to make it better, talking about the striker being a "team player helping others to score goals," and about his "overall contribution to the game," but it doesn't really help the player. He knows. He's there to score goals. That's all that matters. Goals.

Gavin was in the darkest depths of a barren goal-scoring run. He'd been unlucky; he'd seen the ball hit the crossbar, or ricochet from the uprights and crash into the side netting. Goalkeepers had made spectacular saves; defenders had made dramatic goal-line clearances, leaving Gavin desperate and, at times, wondering if he would ever put the ball into the net again. But he had to. He didn't care how—from his feet, from his head, his knee, his chest, anywhere would do. A lucky goal, a fluky goal, he'd even take someone else's deflected shot, as long as the goal was credited to him.

But that goal wouldn't come. He knew full well he was trying too hard; he knew his play was deteriorating, that it was becoming almost embarrassing. But one goal—just one—could change all that.

The Champions League match was against the Norwegian side, Rosenberg. They were no pushovers but just before the interval, after Gavin was brought down just outside the box, David Beckham scored with a trademark, bending free-kick.

The visitors replied soon after the break and from then on both teams had their chances, and several of Real's fell to Gavin. They were no more than half chances, really, but on a good day he would have grabbed one of them. But his hesitant attempts had barely troubled the Rosenberg keeper.

His misery was being compounded by the jeers that had begun to sound from some sections of the Bernabéu whenever he had the ball.

Then another chance came, the best of the lot. Gavin was temporarily unmarked inside the box as he received a through ball from Guti. He just had to swivel and shoot, hard and low. He'd done the same thing thousands of times before; it was easy.

He swiveled, he shot, hard and low, and then he watched the ball miss the target by at least a foot.

The crowd groaned, the whistles echoed around the stadium, and when the substitution board was held up displaying his number, Gavin was not even slightly surprised. As he took his seat on the bench, there was no angry look cast in the direction of Van Der Merwe. Gavin knew the coach was right; he'd deserved to be taken off.

Santiago's elation was equal to Gavin's despair. He was on longer than usual. There was time to settle, to find the rhythm, to be more than just a ten-minute wonder.

He was feeling confident, maybe a little overconfident. He collected the ball close to the halfway line as Real turned defense into attack. There were three of his teammates in excellent positions but instead of making any of the simple passes, he decided to run at the defender closing him down.

It was a bad decision. The nimble defender easily robbed Santiago and sent a long, hopeful ball toward the Real box.

The Real defense was caught flat-footed as Rosenberg counterattacked and only a stunning save from Casillas prevented the visitors from going ahead.

On the bench, Van Der Merwe shouted his fury. "Muñez! Open your eyes! Pass the ball!"

For the first time, Santiago experienced the Madridistas' displeasure as the dreaded whistles came from the terraces. His captain, Raúl, ran over as he walked, head bowed, back to the center circle, and explained in a few short, sharp sentences exactly what was expected of him.

The game restarted and Santiago reminded himself that he was part of a team. Gradually he slipped more comfortably into the pattern of play. He made a couple of good passes and started to link with Ronaldo, but the crowd was growing impatient for the winning goal.

It came with only seconds remaining.

Santiago was the most forward Real player when he collected a probing ball from David Beckham.

This time, he had no option; he had to go for goal. He wrong-footed one defender and then skipped neatly between two more. There was only the keeper to beat and as he advanced quickly, Santiago calmly curled the ball into the net.

On the bench, Van Der Merwe smiled his approval. "Sometimes you don't need to pass."

Santi had done it again—he'd come on as a substitute and scored the winner—and as his name was chanted over and over by the faithful, he joined Ronaldo and Robinho in a samba of celebration.

Back in the dressing room after the final whistle, Van Der Merwe's postmatch summary was not quite so celebratory.

The players sat by their lockers and listened in silence as the coach made his point to them all. "You were taking stupid risks; you could have thrown it away. I told you to control the game, close it down when necessary, but instead you gave me a mountain of unforced errors."

He paused for a moment as the players considered his words. "We were lucky tonight, but if we play second-rate football against Milan, or Liverpool, or Chelsea, they'll bury us."

A few of the squad exchanged looks. They'd won the match; surely they deserved a few words of praise.

Van Der Merwe was quick to sense the mood. "That said, it was a good result, with good goals. And for that, well done."

But the dressing-down wasn't over, for one player, at least. Van Der Merwe's eyes rested on Gavin. "Except for you, Harris. What's going on with you? Are you ever going to score for me again?"

Gavin felt his cheeks redden as his teammates looked away in embarrassment. But he was man enough to admit his failing. He looked back at Van Der Merwe and spoke quietly. "Right now, it doesn't feel like it, boss. Right now, I'm a very bad player."

The coach nodded, surprised at Gavin's unexpected frankness. "Well, I admire your honesty, but I wish you'd told me this before I signed you."

Even Santiago could find no words of comfort for his friend. And besides, he had his own performance and his own place in the Real pecking order to think about.

Footballers can be selfish—in a way, they have to be—and opportunities have to be grabbed when they come along. As Santiago left the dressing room and walked toward the players' exit, he met Van Der Merwe coming in the opposite direction. The coach nodded and walked by, but Santiago had something to say.

"Coach?"

Van Der Merwe stopped and turned back. "Muñez?"

Santiago was nervous but determined to make his point. "I'm fitter than I've ever been. I'm scoring, I'm feeling great."

The coach said nothing—he wasn't making it easy—so Santiago had to continue. He took a deep breath. "I think I'm ready to start a full game."

He'd said it; he'd stated his case, and Van Der Merwe looked at him closely. When he spoke, his words took Santi completely by surprise. "When you're ready, Muñez," he said slowly and deliberately, "I promise, you'll be the first to know."

MUÑEZ—SUPER SUB

Santiago wasn't the first player to be given that title in the newspaper headlines and he wouldn't be the last, but the Madrid press seemed very happy to make him the latest recipient of the honor.

Enrique was sitting in the bar with the back page of the newspaper on the tabletop in front of him as he and a few of the regulars watched a replay of the previous night's wonder goal.

The teenager was supposed to be working, clearing up, doing the jobs that he was routinely meant to do. His father, Miguel, walked in from the room at the back of the bar and scowled as he saw his son staring at the TV set.

"Enrique," he shouted, "go clean out the ashtrays."

Enrique didn't even look away from the TV as he replied, "I'm watching the game."

It was the wrong response. Miguel came storming over and switched off the set. He glared at Enrique. "And when they pay you for watching TV, you'll have a great career. Until then, you roll your sleeves up and get your hands dirty."

He stormed away, leaving Enrique embarrassed and the regulars wondering whether there was time to go to another bar to catch the replays of the postmatch interviews.

14

Roz was at work; it hadn't been the best of days.

She was on her break, deep in thought as she sat on the stairs of the fire escape close to her ward and sipped a comforting cup of tea.

Her cell phone rang and she saw that it was Santiago. She flicked open the phone and answered the call, trying to sound brighter than she felt. "Hi, Santi."

She could hear the roar of an engine as well as Santiago's voice. "You're not going to believe what I just bought us."

Roz couldn't stop herself from sighing. "Go on."

"Guess."

"I don't know, Santi."

Santi wasn't picking up the vibes coming across on the phone.

"Come on, Roz."

"I'm not in the mood for games, Santi."

Santiago obviously was; he was buzzing. "A Lamborghini."

Roz said nothing.

"It's white. A convertible. *So* cool."

There was still no response. Roz took a sip of her tea, as Santiago, at the wheel of his new toy, waited to hear her excited response. It didn't come.

"Roz?"

"Mr. Ives died this morning," said Roz softly.

There was a slight pause before Santiago spoke. "You should have said something."

"You never asked."

"Look, I'm sorry, Roz, really. About Mr. Ives. I know you . . . he was a nice guy. I just wanted to share my news; thought it might brighten your day."

Roz shook her head as she replied. "My day is about as dark as they come, right now. I was going to phone you, just to have someone to talk to. But I didn't want to bring you down, too."

"I'm sorry."

The swing doors to the corridor opened and one of Roz's colleagues poked her head through and gestured that she was needed back on the ward.

Roz nodded. "I've got to go," she said into the phone, and hung up.

The day didn't get better. It was a long, hard shift, and by the time Roz got back to the house that evening she was feeling even more down. And slightly guilty. What did she have to complain about? There was this lovely house in Newcastle, and there was an imposing mansion out in Madrid. She should feel great. Lucky. Privileged. Even grateful.

But she didn't. It was all too strange and unreal, and neither of the houses actually felt like home. She decided to snap herself out of her depression by doing something positive; a bit of do-it-yourself therapy might help. She'd had the paint she'd chosen for the living room for ages. Now was the chance to get it onto the walls.

When her mom, Carol, arrived a couple of hours later, Roz had covered the furniture and carpet with drop cloths and was in the midst of painting the first wall.

Carol didn't offer to help. She'd had her hair done again and was wearing a brand-new pair of snakeskin boots.

She perched on the edge of a drop cloth–covered sofa and watched her daughter painting the wall. "You could pay someone to do that, you know. A professional."

Roz continued rhythmically moving the paint

roller up and down. "I like doing it; makes the place feel more like home."

Carol sighed. She relished her new status of glamorous mother-in-law-to-be of a famous footballer and she didn't want it threatened. And besides, she loved her daughter and she liked Santiago enormously, famous or not. Carol didn't want their relationship to founder but she knew that things were not going well.

"Roz, love," she said gently, "Santi's head is going to be full of a million different things now he's out there in Madrid. You should be one of them, the most important one."

"But I need to be here," said Roz, working faster with the roller. "They need me down at the hospital, and all my friends are here. And even if I was out in Madrid, I wouldn't be allowed to see him. He's in hotels with the team for half the week."

"Not much use having this classy house if it's just you in it, is it though, pet." Carol stood up and walked across the room. She took the paint roller from Roz's hand and turned her daughter around so that she could look into her eyes. "I'm serious, love. It's only a few hundred miles to Madrid, but if you let it, it could become a world away."

She smiled and Roz smiled back, feeling glad that her mom was around to talk to.

Then Carol felt a cold, wet sensation on her right hand. She glanced at the roller; paint was running down the handle and then falling in steady drips. She looked down and saw the splotch of paint on her brand-new snakeskin boots and recoiled in horror.

15

DESPERATE SITUATIONS need desperate remedies and Gavin had decided that his situation was desperate. Training had never been the favorite part of his life as a professional footballer but now he was training harder than ever before.

And not just in the club sessions. In the evenings, he was working like crazy in the gym at his villa. Pumping iron, doing sit-ups, pounding out the miles on the treadmill, riding the stationary bike.

But even at home, as he pedaled the bike and watched a football program on the gym TV, he couldn't escape the pundits' damning verdict as they replayed and discussed his many missed scoring opportunities.

Gavin frowned and pedaled more furiously.

The following day, at official training, he played a practice match as though it were a Cup final. Chasing every ball, diving into the tackle with the enthusiasm of a schoolboy.

He was almost enjoying it, remembering what it was like when he first started to play, until he received a crunching tackle himself and fell heavily. As he lay on the ground, the memory of a thousand similar crunching tackles came flooding back.

Strikers get used to taking more hard knocks than players in the other areas of the field; it goes with the territory. It doesn't mean that the tackles hurt any less, and slowly, but remorselessly, all those tackles take their toll.

But Gavin wasn't going to let it show, not yet anyway. He just grinned as Santiago walked over. He held out his arm so that the young player could haul him to his feet.

After training, Gavin had another massage on his left thigh. It was aching like mad but he tried to ignore the pain by leafing through a magazine as the physical therapist worked on his tortured muscles.

Gavin turned a page and saw the photographs and the caption:

Readers' Phone Poll:
MUÑEZ or HARRIS—Who should START?
YOU DECIDE!

Gavin angrily hurled the magazine toward the trash bin in the corner of the room.

It missed the target.

Santiago was already on the way out of the training complex. The Lamborghini was purring like a contented cat as he eased it toward the main road. He slowed almost to a standstill as he prepared to slip into the line of traffic when suddenly he saw a flash of movement beside the vehicle and felt a thump as something struck the car.

Santiago yelled out in shock. He'd hit someone. He felt his heart pound and then sighed with relief as he saw a scruffy young kid get to his feet and walk round to his side of the vehicle. He had no idea that the accident had been deliberate as the teenager stuck his head into the open window.

"Are you okay?" said Santiago.

"My name is Enrique," said the teenager in Spanish. "I'm your brother."

"What!" said Santiago, completely baffled. "What are you talking about?"

"My mother was married to your father, Herman Muñez. In Mexico City."

Santiago froze, his mouth gaping open, his mind racing.

"I have proof," said the boy.

He pulled an old photograph from his pocket, pushed it through the window, and, when Santiago didn't take it, he dropped it onto his lap.

It was too much for Santiago to absorb and he felt the panic beginning to rise. He shoved the Lamborghini into gear, saw the gap in the traffic, and roared away, leaving the boy watching the vehicle as it disappeared in a cloud of dust.

Santiago drove fast. Too fast. He was sweating, breathing hard, feeling the tightness in his chest. He reached for his inhaler and took a hit. Roz. He had to talk to Roz; she would tell him what to do, how to react.

He grabbed his cell and hit the SPEED DIAL button for the Newcastle house. The phone rang a couple of times and then Santiago heard Roz's voice.

"Sorry, we're out at the moment. Leave us a message and we'll—"

Santiago hit the END CALL button and dropped the phone. He fumbled for the photograph that was still on his lap.

It was a woman. Dark hair. Dark eyes. But could it really, possibly be . . . his mother? Now. After all these years.

He threw the photograph onto the seat next to

him, dropped a gear, and gunned the car down the highway.

When Santiago pulled the Lamborghini into the parking lot of the location of his first TV commercial he was still feeling confused, scared, threatened, and downright angry. The car skidded to a halt, and as Santi opened the door and got out, the commercial's producer came strolling over from a catering truck.

"Santiago." He smiled. "I'm glad you made it. We're ready to start."

The young footballer's usual easygoing and friendly attitude had vanished. "How long will this take?" he snapped.

The producer raised his eyebrows and indicated the way, still smiling but thinking to himself that here was yet another young player who was swiftly growing far too big for his footballing boots.

And it all took far longer than Santiago had imagined. Maybe it was because of his attitude; he was surly and uncooperative from the start, but it was all different and completely new to him.

The setting and costume didn't help. Santi was in a mock-up of a Japanese paneled room with trees and mountains in the background. He was dressed in an orange kimono and was wearing a headband.

Sweltering under the glare of the harsh TV lights, he felt like a complete idiot. He was supposed to look and sound as if he absolutely adored the taste of Total Tofu, but after twenty-six takes he looked as though he would rather die than taste one more mouthful of the stuff.

Santiago's mind was full of the images of the boy at the car window and the photograph, which still lay on the passenger seat. He heard someone shout, "Rolling," and a young guy with a clapper board stood close to his face, snapped the board, and said, "Take twenty-seven," before walking out of shot.

The set went completely silent and then the director, standing behind the camera, looked toward Santi and said, "And . . . action, Santiago."

Santiago was holding chopsticks, and on the table was a plateful of Total Tofu. Santi lifted a small amount to his mouth, chewed it for a couple of seconds, put down the chopsticks, and smiled a cheesy grin straight at the camera.

Then he spoke the words that, after dozens of takes, were imprinted on his brain. "And that's why I go for Total Tofu, every time. Total Tofu, the super-food for the Super Sub!"

He held the cheesy grin for what seemed like agonizing hours until he heard the director shout, "Aaaaaaaand . . . Cut! Lovely. Great."

Santiago spat the rest of the half-eaten tofu into a bucket just out of shot, thinking that at last it was over.

Then the director shouted again, "Let's go for one more."

It was more than Santi could take. He got up from the table, glared at the director, and stormed off in the direction of the makeup room.

The producer turned to the director and sighed. "What's that old saying? Never work with children or animals—or footballers!"

Santiago was staring at his troubled reflection as he held his cell to his ear and waited for the call to be answered. "Come on, pick up. Pick up."

At his workshop in Newcastle, Glen had heard his cell ringing and was wiping his hands on an oily rag as he saw Santiago's name displayed on the phone. He answered the call. "Santiago!"

"This is *not* good, Glen!" yelled Santi into his phone. "These people are making a fool out of me."

"Who, son?" said Glen, taken aback.

"This commercial. David Beckham gets Gillette, and I get freaking tofu!"

Glen was his usual, philosophical self. "It's good money, Santi. And we've got to start somewhere."

"But it's disgusting. Look, why don't you try eating it for five hours straight. I mean, gimme a break here."

"Santi, I'll have a word with—"

"I'm better than this, Glen!" shouted Santiago and then hung up.

Glen stared at his phone, bewildered. Something was wrong. Seriously wrong.

16

THE LAMBORGHINI skidded to a halt outside the house; at this rate it would need a new set of tires before there were a thousand miles on the speedometer.

Santiago got out and went to the front door, his breath shallow and his chest tight. He went inside, taking another hit from his asthma inhaler; he'd used it a lot over the past few hours.

He was about to flick on the lights as he walked into the dining area when he saw the candles on the dinner table. And not just candles; the table was set for dinner, for two.

He stopped and stared, and then he heard a voice coming from the kitchen. "I hope you're hungry."

Roz appeared, holding a spatula and smiling. "I made your favorite."

It was another surprise. A shock. He'd had no idea

that Roz was planning to visit, but this time Santiago couldn't have been happier. He rushed over and hugged her. "You don't know *how* glad I am to see you."

Quickly the story spilled out: the boy at the car, the photograph, and the feeling of panic that Santi had been fighting ever since. Roz listened to every word and looked briefly at the photograph, and then she suggested that maybe they should eat so that Santi could calm himself down before they decided what to do next.

Santi nodded his agreement.

"Good." Roz smiled. "I came a long way to cook this meal."

It was a good suggestion. The food was great, and a couple of glasses of wine helped, too. As they ate, Santi described the agonies of making his first television commercial. And as he relaxed, he was even able to see the funny side of it all.

"This is so good," he said, finishing the last of the chicken Roz had prepared.

"Yeah, I'm sorry it was chicken, but they were all out of tofu down at the shops."

Santiago reacted with mock horror and then his eyes rested on the photograph that sat on the table between them.

Roz picked it up and studied it more closely. "Did the boy say anything else?"

"I dunno. When he threw that at me, I was so freaked I drove off. I couldn't breathe."

"But you always talked about wanting to find her."

"I know, but I can't deal with it now. In my head she was gone forever."

Roz nodded and put the photograph back onto the tabletop. "She does really look like you."

Maybe, thought Santiago, as he looked down at the dark eyes that seemed to be staring back at him. But there was a way of finding out for certain.

In the house in L.A., Santiago's grandmother, Mercedes, stared at the printout of the photograph her grandson had e-mailed to her. She had dreaded this moment for so long.

She picked up the telephone and dialed the number.

Roz was in bed, sleeping, but Santiago was still downstairs, gazing aimlessly at the television. He couldn't sleep until this was sorted out.

He grabbed the telephone at the first ring. "*Sí?*" he said quietly.

"Santiago, where did you get this photograph?"

"Is it her, Grandma?"

There was a silence for a few moments, but the silence only confirmed what Santi had come to believe during the long day and evening.

His grandmother spoke at last. "From the day you went to Spain, I feared this day would come."

"You *knew*! You knew she was here?"

"I couldn't tell you, Santiago. I did not want to cause you pain."

Santi was pacing around the room, not wanting to wake Roz, but his voice hissed with anger. "But she's my mother, and you didn't tell me. My god, Grandma, what gave you the right—?"

"The *right*!" said Mercedes, equally angry now. "That woman left us, Santiago. She just walked away and left your father in pieces. I never saw my Herman smile again; he was empty inside. She broke his heart, Santi, and I swore, the day she left, that I would never let her hurt one of my boys again as long as I lived."

Santiago sat back on one of the sofas and tried to speak more calmly. "But this is my choice, Grandma. She's my mother."

"She abandoned you, Santiago. What kind of woman does that? What right has she now to be back in our lives?"

Santiago sat there for a long time. Thinking. Wondering. Imagining. Trying to drag back into his memory moments from his childhood. Eventually, he fell asleep, but his dreams were troubled and disturbing.

17

VALENCIA: traditionally one of the strongest outfits in La Liga, and with a more than useful campaign under way, a severe examination for Real, even at the Bernabéu.

And in the buildup to the match, Real coach Rudi Van Der Merwe had come under more pressure to give Santiago a place in the starting lineup.

But as Van Der Merwe pondered his decision he had no idea that after weeks of being desperate for a chance of a full ninety minutes in the team, there was suddenly something, or someone, more important than even football at the forefront of Santi's mind: his mother.

During training he'd gone through the motions, putting in the work but with none of the joy he'd felt during his first couple of months at the club.

And when the squad took up its residency at the hotel on the day before the match, he avoided his teammates and took no part in the usual banter and laughter.

As Santiago boarded the bus leaving the hotel for the Bernabéu he felt strangely detached from it all. The supporters were thronging the streets on the approach to the stadium. Chanting. Singing. Santiago heard none of it.

The bus pulled into the shelter of the Bernabéu and as the squad got off and headed quickly toward the double glass and stainless steel doors, which proudly bear the badge of Real Madrid, Santiago suddenly heard his name called from somewhere in the crowd of supporters pressing for a close-up view of their heroes.

"Hey, Santi! Bro! It's me!"

Santiago stopped. His eyes scanned the sea of shouting, laughing, calling faces. And then he saw him. Enrique. The teenager was peering out from the crush of fans, doing his best to wave.

"I need to talk with that kid," said Santiago to one of the security guards, pointing into the crowd.

But it was impossible. The security guard knew his job—he was there to protect the club's multimillion-euro investments, not to fish kids out of the crowd. And besides, he could hardly hear what Santiago was saying. He ushered him forward and Santiago found himself being carried along through the doors and into the relative quiet of the stadium.

Most players find themselves adopting some form of prematch ritual, whether consciously or subconsciously. Some do it for good luck; others do it because they have always done it. The way they undress, or put on their gear; right sock first, or left. The way they tie their shoes; their own particular stretching exercises; the gentle pat of the club badge on their shirt, or the kiss of the necklace. The silent prayer. Every team is made up of individuals, each with their own particular ways.

The Real players were changed and ready. They were watching one of Van Der Merwe's assistants write the names of the starting lineup onto a board.

No one, with the possible exception of the goalkeeper, Casillas, was a guaranteed certainty to start, and even the *galácticos* breathed a little more easily as they saw their names appear.

The assistant had almost finished; Harris was the next name due to appear. Instead, he wrote MUÑEZ.

Only one player reacted; Gavin put on his tracksuit top and walked away. The others remained silent— even the best of them had been there themselves.

Santiago gave no indication of delight, and his teammates probably thought he was being sensitive to Gavin's feelings. But it wasn't that.

Van Der Merwe came into the room and went straight to Santiago. "You're starting tonight, up front with Ronnie."

Santi nodded blankly, almost as though he was in a dream, and Van Der Merwe stared at him for a few seconds, trying to read his thoughts and hoping that the experience of walking out to face Valencia would not prove too overwhelming for the young striker.

During the prematch warm-up, as the stadium filled, Santiago went through his stretching routine. He ran and practiced shots, and even exchanged a few words with other players. But he did all this as though he was on autopilot, as though he would rather be somewhere else. On this, the biggest night of his life.

The team and substitutes went back to the dressing room for Van Der Merwe's final briefing, and then, as kickoff time drew ever nearer, the captain, Raúl, began his own prematch ritual. He slipped on the captain's armband and then, one by one, he kissed each player on the head.

When he reached Santiago he planted the kiss on his head and then whispered quietly, "This is your moment."

Santiago nodded again. He was somewhere else, somewhere a long way away. Ronaldo was sitting next to him, and even a hug of good luck from the smiling Brazilian received no response.

And then they were on their way; through the dressing room doors to the granite steps where the referee and his assistants were waiting. The Valencia players emerged from their own dressing room, and some nodded an acknowledgment to their rivals as they formed their own line on the steps.

The two lines of players began to move, their studs sounding loudly on the stone steps. There were few words now. They walked through the blue covering and out into the glare of the floodlights and the welcoming, ear-blasting roar of eighty-five thousand voices.

The thousands of waving white flags, the ringing cheers and chants, the pounding thump of the drums— they were barely registering for Santiago as he took his place in the lineups across the center circle.

The two teams stood and waved to every side of the stadium, acknowledging the adoration, and then they broke away and jogged into position.

Santiago shook his head. He had to concentrate— he had to focus his mind and give everything for the full ninety minutes.

The referee checked with his two assistants and as he brought his whistle to his lips a sudden hush fell over the Bernabéu. And then the whistle sounded.

Santiago chased and harried for the first couple of minutes but was unable to get even a touch of the ball.

Both teams started cautiously and then, from a Valencia clearance, Santiago collected the ball, thirty-five yards out. He was slow bringing the ball under control and was easily robbed by a Valencia midfielder.

Santi turned to give chase. Like most strikers, tackling was hardly one of the strongest areas of his game, but the tackle he put in from behind was late, high, and dangerous.

The Valencia player went down in a heap and the shrill sound of the referee's whistle cut through the night air. Everyone in the stadium knew that Santiago was about to receive a card; the only question in some minds was which color it would be.

It was red. The referee had no choice; it was a clear decision. Santiago was being sent off after just five minutes. He stood rooted to the spot, unable to believe it had happened. But it had. The Real protests and the whistles from around the ground were pointless.

The Real captain, Raúl, came over to Santiago, sympathetically put an arm on his shoulders, and nodded to him to leave the field.

He forced himself to move, jogging head bowed to the touchline, where he pulled off his shirt and avoided looking toward the bench as he went straight down into the tunnel.

On the bench, Van Der Merwe could hardly contain his fury, but he had to; decisions needed to be made. He nodded toward the coach, Steve McMana-man, and then along the bench to his substitutes.

Real needed to replace the firepower they had lost up front, and in the irony of ironies, Gavin Harris was coming on, so soon after losing his place.

The man to give way was the French midfield mae-stro, Zidane. Gavin was getting another chance.

Santi showered and changed alone, feeling shame, re-morse, regret; a tumble of mixed emotions as he re-lived his moment of madness. He'd let everyone down, the club, his coach, his teammates—and himself. He just wanted to get away from the Bernabéu and the scene of his humiliation as quickly as he could.

He jumped into the Lamborghini, drove it into the dark Madrid streets, and flicked on the vehicle's TV monitor. The match was being broadcast live and ten-man Real was defending manfully against deter-mined opposition.

It seemed almost unbelievable to Santi, as his eyes flicked from the road to the screen, that he was watch-ing the spectacle that he had been part of for those few fateful minutes.

Gavin was playing like a man possessed, going close on goal and helping out in defense as Valencia pushed and harried and strove for a—so far—elusive goal.

Valencia's Uruguayan playmaker, Regueiro, was causing huge problems down the flanks and sending in teasing, wicked crosses, which his teammates had failed to convert, thanks largely to the brilliance of Casillas in the Real goal.

Santiago's dismissal had set the tone for a hard, bruising encounter, but somehow Real was holding on.

It looked as though the match would end goalless, but then, from an increasingly rare Real attack, the ball came into the Valencia box from out wide at no more than waist height.

Gavin was just outside the six-yard box. He flung himself forward, timing his diving header perfectly, and the ball rocketed into the net.

In the car, Santiago smiled for the first time that evening as he heard the match commentator going into raptures over what he called a "great goal."

On the pitch, Gavin was still flat out. He rolled over onto his back, heard the roars of the Madridistas, and smiled up at the night sky.

Teammates came diving in on him, first Robinho, then Raul, then Gravesen, forcing out the last of the breath from Gavin's almost bursting lungs.

But Gavin just laughed. He was back; the goal had come at last.

18

THE BUDDHA BAR is one of Madrid's top nightspots, and a favorite with many of the Real players. It sits in a less than glamorous location by the side of a ring road on the outskirts of the city. But the customers don't go to admire the scenery outside the Buddha; they go for the action.

In the darkened interior, numerous Buddha statues, large and small, stare down with unseeing eyes from every available space. They perch behind the bar, they hover above doorways, and they hide in secluded alcoves, reflecting an aura of tranquillity that contrasts completely with the energy generated by the revelers at the club.

The place throbs with movement and electricity. In the well of the dance floor, beneath the searching, darting glare of strobe lights, hundreds sway to the thudding beat. In the gallery above, groups cluster around low tables, vainly trying to be heard above the pounding music, checking out the fashions worn by others, and casting envious eyes toward the small, roped-off VIP area, where burly security men permit only the chosen few.

All around, waiters and waitresses perform miracles, dodging and weaving between tightly packed bodies, waving arms and outstretched legs as they balance trays full of glasses and bottles on one raised hand with the dexterity of a circus conjurer.

Santiago had not bothered going through to the VIP area. He was sitting at the bar, nursing a beer, having watched Gavin's goal replayed on one of the giant TV screens. The commentator had been right— it was a great goal, and the sense of elation on Gavin's face as the camera zoomed in for a close-up was even greater.

Santi was pleased for Gavin but desperately disappointed for himself. And *in* himself.

As he sipped his beer he saw the glamorous Jordana García gliding toward him.

"Hey," she said. "Hello, hothead."

"Hello, Jordana."

The TV presenter kissed him on both cheeks and then got straight to the point. "It's crunch time, Santi.

I want to interview you on my show while you're still playing for the club."

Santiago almost laughed. "You're not going to give up, are you?"

"At last," said Jordana with a smile. "You realized."

They sat talking together for some time and as they left, the paparazzi were clustered at the exit, cameras poised and ready.

"Can I give you a ride?" asked Santiago as he waited for his car to be brought round from the VIP parking lot.

The white Lamborghini slid to a standstill, and as the car valet got out and held open the driver's door, Santiago looked at Jordana, expecting her to be impressed.

"No thanks, I'm cool." She smiled. She kissed him on both cheeks and the paparazzi cameras flashed, and then she got in behind the wheel of the Lamborghini, just as an identical vehicle pulled up immediately behind the first.

Santiago stared and then smiled as he closed the door of Jordana's vehicle. She looked in her driver's mirror and saw the second vehicle.

"But you do have great taste," she said through the open window before shoving the vehicle into gear and roaring away into the night.

19

SLEEP DIDN'T COME EASILY to Santiago for the next couple of nights.

The sending off troubled him deeply, but not as much as the photograph of his mother. It was a constant reminder that she was there, in Madrid, so close, and yet as far away as she had been for most of his life.

Santi would prowl around the huge house late into the night, trying to picture his mother's life, wondering if he would ever get to meet her. Eventually, he would fall, exhausted, onto one of the sofas and slide into dream-filled sleep.

Roz had managed to get an extra few days in Madrid by swapping shifts with one of her colleagues. She needn't have bothered. Santi was remote and distant, even though Roz was doing her very best to be supportive.

Santi was sleeping soundly on the sofa when she walked in and saw, immediately, the unhappiness etched into his usually sunny features.

"Santi . . ." she said softly, but he didn't stir. Roz knew that he was emotionally drained. She decided to let him sleep for a little longer.

Later she made coffee and prepared fresh orange juice and croissants. She arranged them on a tray, walked into the living room, and set the tray down on the coffee table.

Santiago was still sleeping and Roz went and kissed him lightly on the forehead. "Santi . . ."

He didn't move.

"Santiago, come on, it's late."

He opened his eyes, for a moment not really seeing Roz, or knowing where he was, or quite what was happening. His head was still in his dreams.

And then Roz came into focus and her words registered. "It's late," she'd said. "Any news from your gran?"

But suddenly Santiago wasn't thinking about his grandmother, or his mother, or anything but the time.

He sat up and turned to stare at the clock on the wall. It read 12:50 P.M.

"No!" breathed Santi, leaping from the sofa.

"What?" said Roz.

"Why didn't you wake me?"

"I tried but you were—"

"I'm gonna miss the team plane," yelled Santiago, hurtling up the stairs.

He was back in less than a minute, with a bag in one hand and his Real Madrid blazer in the other. He grabbed his car keys and ran to the door without a word or even a look at Roz.

The front door slammed and a few seconds later Roz heard the roar of the Lamborghini's engine. And then *she* was angry, furious; she didn't deserve to be treated this way. She picked up the tray she had lovingly prepared, hurled it onto the floor, and stomped toward the stairs. So much for her surprise visit. She was going home.

He called to apologize and make his excuses, but there were no excuses. Players just didn't miss the official team plane. Ever.

By the time Santiago had battled his way through the heavy traffic, negotiated temporary roadwork, and found somewhere to park at Barajas Airport, the team flight to Trondheim, Norway, for the return Champions League match with Rosenberg had long since departed.

Problems for Santi begin with a surprise from Enrique . . .

. . . followed
by a cold
ninety
minutes on
the bench
when he
misses the
team plane.

An injury keeps Santi and Roz apart at Christmas—and Santi has other company for the New Year.

Then an accident brings more trouble . . .

. . . and a reunion.

Gavin is back on top!

Who will Burruchaga pick for the final?

A hard fought final . . .

Champions!

The player liaison director, Leo Vegaz, had tersely given Santiago instructions on what he was to do about making his own way to Trondheim when they'd spoken on the phone. Van Der Merwe had been too incensed to even speak to Santiago.

Panting and disheveled, Santi arrived at the ticket counter and slapped down his Platinum AmEx card.

"Trondheim, please," he said in Spanish. "First class."

The desk clerk raised his eyebrows, as if to say, *You'll be lucky, sir,* before replying, "One moment, *señor.* I'll check what's available."

It was easy to become accustomed to first-class air travel. The wide seats, the extra legroom, the obliging flight attendants serving champagne and canapés.

Santiago enjoyed none of that. He was way in the back of the plane, close to the toilets, wedged between a huge American tourist wearing a Hawaiian shirt and a sombrero that he wasn't taking off for anyone, and a puzzled-looking Spanish kid who couldn't quite believe he was sitting next to a real-life Real Madrid player.

The blazer was right and the face was right; he'd seen it enough times on television lately. But what would a superstar be doing stuck back here in coach?

Finally, the kid decided to go for it. He pulled out a pen and took the sick bag from the pocket in the seat in front of him and handed them both, without a word, to Santiago.

Santiago smiled weakly and signed his autograph. He gave the sick bag and the pen back to the boy and then felt the large American nudge him in the side.

"Hey," said the American, as Santi turned to look. "Are you famous?"

Santi smiled again and shook his head.

Leo Vegaz was waiting for Santiago as he emerged from arrivals at Trondheim airport into a bitterly cold day.

"Big trouble," he said to Santiago, ushering him toward a waiting car. "No player has ever missed the team plane before."

"I know," sighed Santi. "I know."

Rosenberg had taken huge encouragement from their performance at the Bernabéu. They had come tantalizingly close to a noteworthy draw and now, on their home field and in conditions they were used to, they were pressing hard for an even more famous victory.

Snow was falling in big flakes, which were picked out in the glare of the floodlights like millions of swirling moths. It was bitingly cold. Up in the stands, Glen, wearing a scarf and his warmest coat, couldn't stop his teeth from chattering.

On the bench, Santiago sat with the other subs, wrapped in layers of Adidas gear. Many of his teammates out on the field were wearing gloves, struggling against the temperature and a team determined to make a little history.

It was hard for the Real players, particularly the Brazilian contingent accustomed to playing their football in a totally different climate, to find their normal rhythm and pace in the icy night air. Gavin Harris was giving his all, hunting down the ball, covering more ground than anyone as he searched for that elusive goal.

The first forty-five minutes had been goalless. Gavin had one fine attempt well saved by the Rosenberg keeper, and in the Real goal, Casillas had pulled off a couple of minor miracles to keep out the opposing strikers.

During the halftime talk, Van Der Merwe hadn't even glanced in Santiago's direction as he encouraged the team to greater effort.

And they were trying harder as the second half progressed, but it was far from easy.

Then, as the Rosenberg defense moved out, Guti played a neat ball through to Gavin. He ran on quickly, like his old self, and sent his shot cleanly and powerfully into the net.

It was there. He'd done it; he'd scored. He raised his arms, he danced for joy, he punched the air.

And then he glimpsed the Rosenberg fans pointing toward the far touchline. He looked back and saw the referee's assistant, still with his flag raised, and he realized that the goal had been disallowed for offside.

It had been a marginal decision, and television replays would show that it was correct, but Gavin couldn't believe his bad luck. It was almost as though he was cursed.

But at least he'd put the ball in the net. He'd done it, he would do it again, and this time the goal would stand.

For the next few minutes, Gavin seemed to almost redouble his efforts, and then, perhaps unsurprisingly, he pulled up sharply as he chased a loose ball.

It was a cramp. An old-fashioned cramp. And it was bad. After a couple of minutes of treatment, the trainer indicated to the coach that it wasn't going to ease quickly and Van Der Merwe had no option but to take off the night's most committed player.

As Gavin hobbled toward the touchline, Van Der Merwe locked eyes with Santiago for a moment and then nodded to one of the other subs to go on.

He looked at Santi again. Words were not necessary.

The match petered out into a goalless draw, and even the Rosenberg players appeared to be pleased to get off the field and back to the warmth of the dressing room and a hot shower. No one was thinking about exchanging shirts as they hurried toward the tunnel.

When Glen went into the dressing room he found Santiago sitting alone on the bench beneath the lockers.

"*Buenos días,* son," he said, getting little more than a nod of acknowledgment in return.

He sat down next to Santiago. "I got a call. There's going to be repercussions; they're talking about a hefty fine." Glen sighed. "Not a day for the memoirs, eh?"

It was as though Santiago hadn't heard. "Zero–zero and he had me sitting on my freezing backside for ninety minutes."

"He's the coach; it's his call. He's sending you a message, Santi, and you need to listen."

Santiago turned and glared at his agent, his friend, the man responsible for giving him the opportunity to turn his lifelong dream of becoming a professional footballer into reality. But all that was far from his mind as he spoke. "Don't patronize me, Glen. I'm doing commercials for tofu while you're fixing cars in Newcastle."

"I'm only a flight away, son," said Glen. He'd never seen Santiago like this before. "And I came as soon as they called."

"Yeah, well, I need someone full-time, Glen. In Madrid, to support me off the field."

Glen could see the direction the conversation was taking. "Perhaps this is where I get off then."

The argument wasn't about tofu commercials, or opportunities that needed to be seized. Glen knew that perfectly well. There was something more troubling Santiago—something unspoken that was hurting him deeply, something that was forcing him to take out his anger and frustration on his closest friend and staunchest supporter.

Glen held out his hand. "It's been a great ride, Santi. A privilege."

Santiago took Glen's hand and shook it. But he didn't look at him. He couldn't; they both knew that it was the end.

The disappointment and hurt showed clearly on Glen's face as he turned away and walked to the door. Then he stopped and looked back. "You know, your plate's getting so full so fast, son. You should watch what falls off the edge."

He turned away and walked through the door, leaving Santi still staring at the floor.

20

SANTIAGO HAD ARRIVED BACK from Trondheim to find the house horribly empty. Roz had pinned the briefest of notes to the fridge door before leaving.

Since then he hadn't spoken to her by phone. Or to Glen. He didn't know what to say to either of them.

Each day he'd arrived at training hoping to see the young kid, Enrique, again. There was so much more he needed to know now.

But if Enrique was there, Santiago didn't spot him.

And so he'd spent the evenings moping around the house, watching television alone, thinking about calling Roz or Glen and then deciding against it, and staring at the photograph. Of his mother.

Gavin had had a terrific night, but as far as Gavin was concerned, the night was still young.

He drove back to his villa with two girls from the Buddha Bar. They got out of the car, giggling, and stumbled up to the front door.

Gavin slid his key into the lock, whispering to the girls in appalling Spanish, and found that the key wouldn't turn. He frowned, pulled out the key and gave it an accusing stare, and then tried again. It still wouldn't turn.

The girls were becoming impatient; it was cold at that hour of the morning and their flimsy outfits were not exactly suited to a late-night wander around the garden.

Gavin trampled over the nearest flower bed and went to the large picture window which spread across most of the living room. He cupped his hands to the glass and peered inside. For a moment he thought he'd been robbed, but *everything* was gone. All he could see were a few black garbage bags, stuffed full with clothes—his clothes.

"Oh, no!"

One of the Spanish girls tapped him on the shoulder. She was holding an envelope she had found pinned to the bottom of the door. Gavin ripped open the envelope and, peering closely in the darkness, read the letter that was inside.

"What!"

The girls stared at him; this wasn't the way they were expecting the night to continue.

"We have to go. Where do you live? I'll have to take you home."

Their English was no better than Gavin's Spanish; they were totally confused. Gesturing with both hands, Gavin ushered them back to the car and they got in. He started the engine and drove quickly away, listening to the girls speaking loudly to each other as they tried to figure out what was going on.

"I've been evicted," he said when the opportunity to get a word in eventually came. "Evicted! You understand? How do you say *evicted*?"

The girls didn't understand, but one of them answered Gavin with a few quick words, making him mistakenly think that she knew what he was saying.

"Yeah, that's it, right. They've repossessed the property, thrown me out. I owe money." He could see them looking at him blankly, so he attempted a mixture of Spanish and English. "*Dinero!* I have *no más dinero! Nada!*"

The girls' look of confusion turned to one of fury, and one of them began to yell in Spanish. This time she had jumped to the wrong conclusion. "You think we want *money* to go back to your house! What the hell do you think we are?"

Gavin didn't understand a word, so he just blustered on. "My agent. Barry scumbag Rankin. He had me invest in some bogus vineyard in France for my pension. *Sí? Comprende?* I have nothing left! Nothing!"

"*Stop!*" screamed the girl, who still thought Gavin was talking about paying them for the pleasure of their company.

"What? Stop? Here? Why?"

"*Yes!*"

The car screeched to a standstill and the two girls got out, screaming at Gavin and slamming the door so hard that it made him shudder.

As he drove away he could still hear their yells.

It was almost dawn when Santiago was woken from a troubled sleep by the sound of the door buzzer. He got out of bed, and wearing just his boxer shorts, he padded over to the videophone and pressed a button.

Gavin's grinning face came into view on the small, black-and-white monitor.

"Any room at the inn?" he said.

Santiago knew that after the Trondheim incident and his shameful actions in his fleeting appearance in the Valencia match he would have to work doubly hard to regain Van Der Merwe's confidence. And before he could even be considered for team selection he had to serve a suspension.

But his head wasn't right. As Roz wouldn't return his calls and he'd split with Glen, there was only his new houseguest, Gavin, to talk to. And although Gavin was great for a laugh, Santiago wasn't in the mood for laughs.

He would rather have been alone, but he couldn't refuse his friend. After all, Gavin had taken him in when they were both at Newcastle.

Santiago was hoping that it would be a short-term arrangement, but he wasn't encouraged when he asked Gavin how long he thought he would be staying.

Gavin just shrugged and said, "Quite a while, I reckon."

When he went on to explain the extent of his financial problems, thanks to the expert advice of Barry Rankin, Santiago realized that he really was in for the long haul. And Gavin wasn't the easiest houseguest; he was more like a big kid who needed a lot of looking after. But at least he was never boring and eventually Santiago decided that he just had to get on with things.

But the thought that his mother and half brother were out there somewhere in Madrid was with him all the time.

He stayed low-key at training, putting in the work and sticking to the rules. There were plenty of stories of players who'd upset the boss and then spent the remainder of the season out in the wilderness, omitted from the first-team squad before being shipped out of the club during the next transfer window. It was the nightmare scenario, but even at Real Madrid, no player was bigger than the club.

In the following league game, Gavin scored again in an impressive Real performance. Despite his financial woes, he appeared to be back to his irrepressible best, even off the field.

One evening, he was down in the huge basement parking area at Santi's house, playing "keep-up" with a football.

Santiago walked down the stairs; he'd been trying to get through to Roz on the phone. "She won't speak to me. I don't know why she's so angry."

Gavin flicked the ball up onto his thigh and then knocked it over to Santi.

"Well, I can understand. She's there all alone," said Gavin, grinning as Santi juggled the ball on his instep a few times before sending it back down the hallway. "While you're out with dark-haired Spanish beauties."

"But I'm not out with dark-haired Spanish beauties," said Santiago as the ball came back.

Gavin watched as Santi demonstrated a few of the skills he'd learned from the Brazilians at Real, juggling the ball between instep, thigh, heel, and shoulder.

"Yeah, very good, but you've still got some serious groveling to do, my son."

The ball was returned faster and Gavin took it on one thigh. He let it drop to his instep and then flicked it up so that he could head it back toward Santi. Gavin wasn't famed for his heading ability and the ball went high to Santi's left.

He instinctively moved back to stop it. He didn't see the bicycle lying on the cement floor. His left foot twisted in the spokes of one of the wheels and Santi went down with a yell.

Gavin stared as Santi lay sprawled across the bicycle, flinching in pain as he reached down to his injured leg.

"Come on, stop messing around," said Gavin, walking over to Santi.

Santi looked up at him. "This is serious, man. It really hurts."

They say that bad things come in threes. Valencia had been bad, Trondheim had been even worse, and the broken bone in his foot completed the most unwelcome hat trick of Santiago's brief career.

Van Der Merwe went ballistic. The injury meant

that Santi would be out of action for at least ten weeks. He would miss a vital chunk of the season—important league games, the remaining Champions League group matches, and well into the knockout phase.

The furious coach banned his player from going anywhere but the training ground or his home. And when Santiago told him that he had been planning to return to England for Christmas, the coach replied with just two words: "Forget it!"

Santiago's one consolation was that when Roz heard about the injury—from Gavin—she did at least agree to speak to him on the phone.

The conversation began well enough. Roz was sympathetic; being a nurse she'd seen and dealt with far more serious injuries, but she did her best to sound concerned and understanding.

Santiago was at home, lying on the sofa, with his leg up and his foot in a bright blue orthopedic boot. A pair of crutches rested against one of the other chairs.

They had been chatting for about five minutes when Santiago took a deep breath and finally told Roz that Van Der Merwe had banned him from traveling home for Christmas.

There was a moment of stunned silence. "But he can't do that," said Roz at last. "I've got everything planned. Jamie and Lorraine are coming round with little Keanu. My mum's doing the turkey."

"I know. And all I want is to be with you, now, at home. I feel like I'm under house arrest."

"But I don't understand. What's the point in them keeping you over there? You can't even do any training."

Santiago shifted uncomfortably on the sofa as he felt a painful twinge in his foot. "They pay me, Roz; they call the shots. I'm sorry, I can't change that."

Roz couldn't hold back her anger. "I can't believe this. You promised. It's not fair and it's not that much to ask. All the times I've been over to Madrid and you've not come home once, Santi, you've not even set foot in Newcastle. You *said* we'd have Christmas together."

"Roz, it's out of my hands. I—"

"*No,*" said Roz, interrupting. "It's just another excuse. If you hadn't sacked Glen he could have sorted it out. Well, I'm getting sick of it, Santi. *Sick* of it!"

She hung up and Santiago flinched as another stab of pain jarred through his foot.

21

REAL MADRID SAFELY, if unspectacularly, negotiated the group stages of the Champions League, but even before Christmas it looked unlikely that the club would add to its tally of twenty-nine league titles.

Barcelona already looked well set to retain the title, although outsider Osasuna was putting up a spirited challenge.

Gavin was training furiously and playing well in a team that wasn't quite firing on all cylinders, while Santiago could do nothing but sit and watch and wait impatiently for his injury to heal.

He spoke to Roz several times and appealed to Van Der Merwe to change his mind about letting him return to England. But there was no shifting the coach; he wanted his troublesome striker where he could see him, believing that he could still play a significant part in the closing weeks of the season—if he could regain his fitness and if he could stay out of trouble.

Santiago was dreading Christmas Day, and when it arrived it was as gloomy and depressing as he had feared.

He called his grandmother and brother in L.A. and then he called Roz, who chatted brightly as she described the Christmas Day she was spending with her mom and their friends, Jamie and Lorraine and their new baby.

She told him about the presents, the decorated tree, the Christmas lunch with crackers and paper hats. "Little Keanu loves the lights on the Christmas tree. He's such a beautiful baby. Pity he looks like Jamie."

She was doing her best to sound cheerful, but Santiago knew that behind the jokes and laughter, Roz was just feeling as lonely as he was.

Later, as he and Gavin shared a Christmas dinner of take-out Chinese food straight from the boxes, Santi found himself wondering about his other family, his mother and his half brother. How, he wondered, were they spending their Christmas Day? Were they thinking of him, too?

They were, although neither of them mentioned it to the other. Enrique's father, Miguel, had surprised his son by giving him a Christmas present of a brand-new football. It was an uncharacteristic gesture of kindness from Miguel, who had even gone to the trouble of wrapping the ball in paper.

Rosa-Maria sat with her husband and watched Enrique unwrap the present. His eyes widened in delight as he saw the football and he smiled his thanks to his father. Then he looked at his mother.

He knew then that as she watched him holding the ball, she was thinking of Santiago, just as she knew that he was thinking of Santiago.

But Miguel knew nothing of their thoughts. Rosa had never told him about the existence of her two other sons, Santiago and Julio; she had been afraid of his response. And now, when she wanted to tell him, she feared that it was far too late.

At Santiago's house, Gavin finished the last of his steamed chicken with noodles and licked his lips.

He glanced over at the glum-faced Santiago and sighed. Santi needed cheering up.

"Right, then," said Gavin. "Fancy a game of charades?"

When New Year's Eve arrived, Madrid was covered in a blanket of snow. It made Santiago even more depressed.

Gavin had moved on from charades and party games to organizing the sort of party he preferred. He'd arranged for a few of the Real players and their wives or girlfriends, along with some other close friends, to come over to the house to see in the New Year. And like all Gavin's get-togethers, he'd invited a few extra girls, just so that he didn't get lonely.

As the party got into full swing downstairs, Santi went up to his room, to leave a message on Roz's phone.

He knew that Roz was working, and as she'd be midway through a late shift on a busy ward, there would be no way she could take a call as midnight approached in Madrid. So Santi's only option was to leave a message.

"Hey, Roz. I can't believe we're not together on New Year's Eve. I'll make it up to you, I promise." He paused for a moment. There was a lot more he wanted to say but it wasn't the moment; it would have to wait until the next time he saw her. "I love you, Roz. Happy new year."

He ended the call and eased himself up, grabbing the two crutches that had become like two friends who had long outstayed their welcome, and moved cautiously over to the window. Snow was covering the parked cars and Santi stood staring into the darkness until the sound of the party downstairs broke into his thoughts.

Midnight was getting nearer and Santi realized that as the party was at his house, he should at least be downstairs with his guests to see in the new year. But crutches and an orthopedic boot hardly helped with the party mood.

He hobbled down the stairs to be met by one of the late arrivals—Jordana. She greeted him at the foot of the stairs with a bottle of opened champagne in each hand.

"Why the long face, Santi?" She smiled. "It's party time!"

Carefully she led him to where the partygoers were dancing before raising one of the champagne bottles to his mouth so that he could take a drink.

"Come on, let's dance."

It wasn't exactly dancing, but Santiago did clump around on his crutches as best he could as his dancing partner gave him more champagne.

As the last seconds of the old year ticked away, Gavin, unsurprisingly accompanied by two girls, led the countdown to midnight.

"TEN . . . NINE . . . EIGHT . . . SEVEN . . ."

More voices joined in the countdown chorus as Jordana moved closer to Santiago.

"SIX . . . FIVE . . . FOUR . . ."

Santi knew exactly what Jordana had in mind; it was the new year and a kiss was the tradition.

"THREE . . . TWO . . . ONE . . . *FELIZ AÑO NUEVO! HAPPY NEW YEAR!*"

The yells and cheers rang around the room, along with the usual hugs and kisses.

And Jordana kissed Santiago, gently at first. Then she stood back for a moment and stared deeply into his eyes. She moved back and kissed him again. But this time the kiss was long and passionate.

Santiago woke up late the following morning. He lay on his bed, his head thumping, and slowly the events of the previous night came back into his mind. Or some of them.

He stared at the ceiling for a few long minutes before gradually easing himself into a sitting position, putting his head into his hands to try to stop the pounding in his brain.

Without thinking, Santi threw his leg off the bed to get up and was instantly rewarded with a jolting reminder of his broken foot as pain seared up through his leg. He gasped and fell back on the bed, deciding that further movement wasn't a good idea for the next few minutes.

Gavin was sitting at the kitchen table eating from a bowl packed with cereal, yogurt, and fruit when Santi finally hobbled in on his crutches. He watched, but said nothing as Santi went to the fridge and opened the door.

Santi took a long drink and stared out through the window at the snow. When he turned back he saw that Gavin was watching him.

"What?"

Gavin shook his head and went back to his breakfast.

"What?" said Santi again.

"I didn't say anything," said Gavin through a mouthful of cereal.

"But you were looking at me, with a . . . *look*."

"No, I wasn't."

They stared at each other, Gavin silently challenging his friend to make his confession. But Santi decided that it was probably wisest to say no more. He shrugged irritably and then hobbled back to the kitchen door.

"Nothing happened," he called as he went out.

Gavin smiled but didn't reply.

A few seconds later Santiago came back into the room. "*Nothing* happened!"

22

IT WAS FALLING APART. His career. His life. Santiago felt that everything was spiraling downward, out of control. And the only way he could stop the downward spiral and start rebuilding his future was to discover the truth about his past.

He'd talked it over with Gavin, who'd been a surprisingly good listener after all. Santi showed him the photograph of his mother and told him of his meetings with his half brother, and Gavin had agreed that the only way to deal with the situation was by confronting it.

But that wasn't easy. Santiago had no idea where his mother was living, and he hadn't seen Enrique again.

Even though he was still wearing the plastic boot, Santiago was attending training every day. He did light gym work to maintain his upper body strength and received expert treatment and physiotherapy to his injured foot.

He could even drive, with care.

Each time he arrived and left the training facility he looked for Enrique, and finally, as he drove off at the end of a session, he saw him at the edge of the crowd.

Santiago pulled the vehicle to a halt and pressed the button to open the passenger-side window. "You want a lift?"

Enrique raised his eyebrows and then turned and smiled at the crowd gathered around the exit, looking as though catching a ride with a Real Madrid player was something that happened to him all the time.

He got in and Santiago drove away.

They didn't speak for a while. Santiago was unsure of what to say and Enrique was too fascinated and enthralled by the ultracool vehicle.

He pushed every button there was on the satellite navigation system and grinned with delight at the graphics.

"Hey," he said at last. "If I had one of these, I'd get respect. I'd drive to the ocean, man, and never come back."

He explored the glove box and then checked out the CDs, frowning at Santiago's taste in music.

"Take this left," he said as they approached one of the run-down areas of the city. Santiago did as he was instructed, thinking that perhaps Enrique was taking him to his home. And their mother.

The teenager grabbed Santi's phone and the spare pair of sunglasses he kept in the glove box. "How d'you work the camera on this phone?"

He didn't wait for an answer; the camera on the phone was easy enough to operate. He slipped on the shades and snapped a photograph of himself and then grinned at the results.

"Next right."

The vehicle slid smoothly into a district unknown to Santiago, with narrow streets and shabby, neglected buildings. The few people out on the streets stared in surprise as the Lamborghini rolled by and Enrique beamed at them through the tinted windows.

He started flicking through the speed dial list on Santi's cell and then hit a number. "Hey, Mr. Van Der Merwe, you wanna give me a trial? I'm much better than my big brother."

Santiago snatched the phone away, horrified. He cut the call, relieved to see that it had gone un-answered.

"Just stop it, will you?" he said to Enrique.

Enrique eased himself back in the seat, wondering what he could do next.

"Tell me about your mother," said Santiago.

The youngster shrugged. "What's there to tell? She gives me a hard time, so I stay away as much as I can."

It wasn't the answer Santi had been expecting and he was still trying to work out his next question when Enrique pulled Santi's sports bag from the rear seat and began rifling through it.

"This is really cool," he said, examining the Adidas gear in the bag.

Santiago stopped the car as a traffic light turned to red and then watched as one of his sweatshirts dropped from the bag onto the floor of the car.

"Look, will you sit still! What's your problem, man?"

Enrique turned on him angrily. "You want to know my problem? I'll tell you. I live in a rotten place, my mom works herself into the ground, and you're driving around in this like some sort of movie star. That's my problem!"

Before Santiago could reply, his half brother threw open the passenger-side door, leaped from the vehicle, and ran off down the street, with Santiago's sports bag in one hand.

"*Hey!*" yelled Santi, struggling to get out of the car. There was no way he could give chase; he couldn't risk damaging his injured foot any further, and the plastic boot wasn't going to give him any help even if he tried.

He saw Enrique disappear down an alleyway and then heard the sound of a car horn as the traffic light turned to green.

He looked back and glared at the driver of the vehicle behind him. The driver raised both hands and gestured for Santi to get his car moving.

"All right!" shouted Santiago. "I'm going!"

Enrique's new football sat on his bed. He was hurriedly stuffing the sports gear he'd stolen from Santiago beneath the bed when his mother came into the bedroom. She didn't knock; she'd seen him run quickly across the bar with the bag.

"What did I tell you about stealing?" she said furiously as Enrique turned toward her.

"I didn't steal it. Santi gave them to me."

Rosa's eyes widened. She closed the bedroom door quietly and grabbed her son by the shoulders. "Santiago? Are you insane? I told you we can never be part of his life."

"But he's my brother!" snapped Enrique, trying to pull himself free. "Why is this something I have to hide?"

"Because . . ." They both knew why, but Rosa-Maria couldn't bear to say the words. Instead, she slapped her son across the face. "In this house, you do what you are told!"

Before Enrique could argue back, the door opened and his father came in.

"What the hell is going on?"

Rosa-Maria released her grip on Enrique. She stared at him, her eyes making a silent appeal to keep their secret.

Enrique looked at his mother with contempt. Then he snatched his football from his bed, brushed quickly past his mother and father, and ran down the stairs.

"Well?" said Miguel to Rosa-Maria.

"He's . . . he's . . ."

She stooped down and pulled the sports bag from beneath the bed. "He's been stealing again."

Enrique hadn't gone far—he'd headed for the bare patch of ground where he and his friends usually played their pickup games of football. But Tito was the only one there. He was throwing stones at a huge billboard when he saw Enrique approaching with his new football.

He grinned. "Nice ball."

Enrique nodded proudly and handed over the ball when Tito held out both hands.

The older boy inspected the ball carefully and bounced it on the ground a couple of times. Then, before Enrique could stop him, he drew back his right foot, dropped the ball, and volleyed it as hard as he could.

Enrique gazed in horror as the ball sailed away through the air and over a high wall that bordered the makeshift football field. The ball was gone. Forever.

Enrique's eyes blazed with fury and he leaped at the smirking Tito, throwing wild punches into his body and at his face. But the bullying Tito was not only older and bigger than Enrique, he was also a lot stronger.

He grabbed the smaller boy's flailing arms and in one swift, brutal move, he lifted him off the ground and slammed him down in the dirt. He laughed once and then strolled away, oblivious to the tears in Enrique's eyes.

23

EL CLÁSICO—the classic. It isn't a local derby because the two teams are from completely different regions of Spain. But it is the big one, for both Real Madrid and Barcelona, and for their supporters.

The two clubs are traditionally Spain's biggest and bitterest of rivals. Their encounters spark hundreds of column inches of speculation and comment in the press and hour upon hour of coverage on television and radio. The buildup begins weeks before the match and always leads to fierce debate.

There are plenty of British matches that annually ignite old rivalries: Glasgow's old firm battle between Rangers and Celtic; the clash of the Lancashire giants, Manchester United and Liverpool; the north London derby between Tottenham and Arsenal; but even these do not quite compare. In Italy there is Milan's Inter versus AC. All over Europe and throughout the footballing world there are certain matches that fire the imagination and the passion of players and supporters alike.

But something, somehow, sets Real Madrid versus Barcelona apart. It is *the* one. The ultimate encounter. It is simply *El clásico*.

The *galácticos* of Madrid were matched by the superstars of Barcelona, Deco, Messi, Eto'o, and, of course, the man voted as the very best player in the world, the sublimely skilled Brazilian, Ronaldinho.

The Barcelona maestro, Ronaldinho, gives names to the best of his magical tricks with a football. He calls one "The Chewing Gum" because the ball appears to be stuck to his feet.

As the match progressed, the lithe Brazilian displayed his full repertoire of brilliance, beguiling the Real defenders and bringing grudging appreciation from even the partisan Madridistas.

Ronaldinho, ably assisted by the young Argentinian, Messi, was creating havoc in the Real defense.

But then close to the end, and against the run of play, there was a moment of joy for Real, and for one player in particular. But Barca wasn't having it all their own way, and one Real player in particular was demonstrating exactly why so many clubs had paid so much money for his skills during his long career.

Gavin was having a blinder, and enjoying every

second of it. And the much-traveled and much-maligned striker's joy was complete midway through the second half when, from a pass across the face goal from outside the area, he was there to skillfully side-foot the ball into the net.

All the missed chances, the fluffed kicks, the bad matches, were instantly forgotten by the wildly celebrating Madridistas. Gavin had scored in *El clásico*.

He was a hero again.

Santiago and Jordana sat opposite each other in comfortable chairs on the classy set of her TV show.

The television crew bustled around, making their final preparations for the show, which was broadcast live every day. They ignored Santi and Jordana; everyone had a job to do and the added pressure of a live broadcast meant split-second timing, which left no room for errors.

It was the first time Santi had seen Jordana since their encounter on New Year's Eve, and while she was her usual smooth, sophisticated self, he was feeling edgy and a little embarrassed.

Jordana was partly amused at her guest's nervousness, but she was in work mode; the show and the interview were what mattered most.

She spoke softly in her native Spanish, seeking to

put Santiago more at ease in the unfamiliar surroundings of the studio. "You must be dying to play again."

Santiago shrugged self-consciously, for the moment avoiding eye contact with the superconfident presenter. "Yeah, it won't be too long now," he replied, slipping easily into Spanish himself.

"I'm glad you're finally here, giving me the exclusive."

"Sure, no problem," said Santi, halfheartedly.

It was hardly the dynamic attitude that Jordana was looking for.

"Listen," she said firmly. "I hope you're going to give me a juicy interview?"

Santiago lifted his eyes and glanced around the studio. No one was paying them the slightest attention. "Yeah, I'm okay with you torturing me in front of the world on TV, as long as what happened between us stays between us."

Jordana smiled. "You're only keeping your promise. And let me give you the benefit of my experience, Santi. Nothing in life is free. The sooner you learn that, the better it will be for you."

"What happened between us was a mistake," said Santi, quietly but urgently. "I was drunk, and very lonely. I'm not like that."

Jordana knew exactly how to push Santi into the

mood she wanted for the show. "Look, Santiago, if you don't want to be treated like a child, behave like a man. What happened, happened."

Santi's eyes flashed. "That's right. And I'm here to make sure things are clear. It'll never happen again."

She'd done it, sparked up her guest into a fiery mood, exactly how she wanted him and at exactly the right time. "Very good. Priorities right, eyes on the ball. Now, Santi, just give me a great interview!"

The studio floor manager got the thumbs-up from the control gallery and began the countdown to the show, both verbally and by using the fingers of his right hand to count off the final five seconds. They were about to go live.

"Three . . . two . . . one . . ." He pointed at Jordana; they were on the air.

She beamed into the camera. "Hello and welcome. Today I have the honor of having here as my very special guest, Real Madrid's new star player, Santiago Muñez."

24

EMINEM WAS PUMPING from the Lamborghini's sound system as Santiago pulled into the driveway at the Buddha Bar.

He got out and nodded to the valet waiting to take the vehicle round to the parking area. A few of the paparazzi were lurking by the entrance, as usual, on the hunt for that big moneymaking photograph.

"Oi, Muñez," called one, in English. "You gonna show us that fiery Mexican temper of yours again?"

The comment was designed to provoke Santi into an outburst of anger, but it didn't succeed. So the photographer tried again. "Hope you liked the photo spread in *Heat* magazine!"

Santi glanced at the smirking Englishman but continued into the club and the disappointed photographer turned to one of his colleagues and shrugged his shoulders. "Worth a try."

Several of the Real players were already in the club. A huddle of defenders—Salgado, Helguera, and Jonathan Woodgate—were clustered around a table along with Gavin.

When Santi finally made it through to his teammates, Salgado stood up and held out his cell phone. "Hey, Santi, what's going on? This is the third time you've called me."

Santiago frowned. He hadn't called Salgado once, let alone three times. He checked through his pockets and quickly realized that he must have left his phone in the car.

His car!

He grabbed Salgado's phone, put it to his ear, and immediately heard the Eminem CD he had been playing when he arrived.

Someone was in his car!

He shoved Salgado's phone back into his hands and turned back toward the entrance, pushing his way through the hordes of startled clubbers.

The paparazzi were still keeping their vigil as Santi emerged from the club and ran up to the parking valet.

"Where's my car?" he said urgently.

"In the car park, sir. Round at the back."

"Show me!"

Before they had taken more than a few steps, the Lamborghini came skidding around the side of the club and Santiago saw with horror that Enrique was behind the wheel. The teenager gave his half brother the single-finger gesture as the car flashed by and onto the road.

Santi tore out in pursuit. A taxi was approaching the club, the driver looking for the early departures from the Buddha. He wasn't expecting to see a young man standing directly in his path in the middle of the road, frantically waving both hands to flag him down.

As the cab skidded to a halt, the English photographer fumbled for his own keys and ran back to the parking lot.

The elderly taxi driver stuck his head out of the window and yelled at Santiago. "You lunatic! You got some kind of death wish?"

There was no time to argue. Santi wrenched open the passenger door and leaped into the beaten-up old Škoda, pointing toward the taillights of the Lamborghini.

"That's my car! Don't let it out of your sight!"

The cabdriver's eyes narrowed and his neck craned forward as he stared into the darkness; he could just see the back of the high-performance car weaving from side to side along the long stretch of road.

"You want me to . . . ?"

"The white Lamborghini, yes!"

"A *Lamborghini*! In *this*?"

"Yes! Follow that car!"

The old cabdriver grinned an almost toothless grin. For years he'd been waiting to hear those words. He crossed himself, pulled his bifocal glasses down from the top of his head and jammed them into place, and then shoved the Škoda into gear.

The tires screeched as it pulled away and the cabdriver's smile was even wider as he burned rubber for the first time in his life.

A few seconds later, the English photographer emerged from the lot perched on a Lambretta scooter, which whined like an out-of-control lawn mower as the paparazzi man also gave chase.

25

ENRIQUE WAS NO GRAND PRIX RACER, but then the Lamborghini was hardly designed for a driver of his size. Even with the seat moved fully forward, his feet barely reached the pedals, and as he drove he constantly had to raise himself up to see over the steering wheel.

Going in a straight line was not too difficult, as long as he didn't try to go too fast, but rounding a corner was a completely different matter.

Once he got off the ring road, the real problems began. He rounded a corner too quickly and almost lost control as he saw the roadwork up ahead. Late. Too late.

Traffic cones scattered like bowling pins in every direction as he plowed through them, and at the next bend an oncoming car had to swerve violently to avoid the Lamborghini.

Enrique saw the flashing headlights and heard the blaring horn, but only glimpsed the vehicle as it swept by. Then he heard the crash as the other car hit a recycling bin by the roadside. But Enrique didn't slow down.

The old taxi driver did, but only long enough to check that the driver of the crashed car was unhurt. As soon as Santiago saw him emerge from his battered vehicle, he urged the driver on.

"Stay with him, but don't spook him."

"But I can catch him," said the driver, enjoying every second of the drama. "Just give me a chance."

"No. Follow him. That's all."

The taxi driver squinted through his bifocals; maybe it was more like the movies just to follow. But that didn't mean he couldn't edge a little nearer.

They were traveling into the city center and the traffic was getting heavier, making Enrique's struggle to keep the Lamborghini under control even more difficult. The slightest pressure on the accelerator sent it rocketing forward.

He reached an intersection and cut directly across the path of a line of cars, causing the driver of the first to brake violently. The two following vehicles had no chance to stop and Santi and the taxi driver passed seconds later and saw the tangle of smashed headlights and bent fenders.

As the old Škoda drew closer to the Lamborghini, the taxi driver craned forward again and squinted through his glasses.

"There's no one driving it!"

Just then, Enrique's hand emerged from the window again and he gave another single-finger gesture.

The taxi driver shrugged. "It's a little guy."

Enrique was beginning to panic; he hadn't expected his joyride to turn into a chase. He had sneaked into the parking lot and had been amazed to find the vehicle unlocked with the keys still in the ignition. He slipped into the car and fooled around with Santi's cell phone for a while, loving the way he could pretend for a few minutes that the Real Madrid stars on the speed dial were *his* friends. And then, impulsively, he decided on a quick joyride; now he had to get away while he could. He hit the brakes and wrenched the wheel hard to his right, swerving into a side street. But the pursuing taxi stayed with him.

The teenager put his foot down, going too fast for the narrow road. He took another corner and the back end of the vehicle fishtailed, taking out wing mirrors and denting the paintwork of a couple of parked vehicles.

Enrique was losing control, but in his panic he kept his foot down hard on the accelerator pedal. He clipped a parked motorbike on his left-hand side and then saw the bend ahead as he wrestled with the wheel, jerking it right, to left, and back again.

He had no chance of making the turn. As the car slewed round, Enrique saw the newsstand; he was going to hit it. He closed his eyes, tightly, instinctively. He heard the terrifying noise at the moment of impact.

And then darkness closed in and he felt or heard nothing more.

The taxi rounded the corner and screeched to a standstill. Santi leaped from the vehicle and tore over to the wreckage of the Lamborghini, crunching over broken glass and breathing dust as he wrenched open the buckled driver's door.

Enrique was slumped forward over the steering wheel, his head cut and bleeding badly.

"Enrique!"

There was no response. Gently Santiago eased his half brother back in the seat. His eyes were closed and his face was deathly pale.

"Enrique!"

Santiago saw that his hands were still shaking as he gripped the plastic cup of steaming, vending machine coffee.

He was sitting in the hospital waiting room, and the questions being fired at him from the two police officers as they adopted the good-cop/bad-cop routine were not helping one bit.

"And you say you just lost control?" said Bad Cop.

"I told you, I was distracted, my cell phone rang. I know I should have ignored it."

"And the boy with you?"

"A friend's son. I already told you that, too."

The officers exchanged a look; the story didn't ring true to either of them.

The old taxi driver had been a hero, forcing his ancient Škoda into a lightning drive, through back streets and shortcuts to the hospital.

Santiago ran into the emergency room with the bleeding Enrique in his arms and the expert staff moved swiftly and efficiently into action.

The last Santiago had seen of his brother was when a doctor hurried into the treatment cubicle as nurses checked for pulse and blood pressure. Santiago was ushered away to the waiting room where he had prepared his story for the police.

It had seemed the best thing to do, for Enrique's sake, but the story wasn't going down well.

"The boy is knocked about pretty bad," said Bad Cop.

"He didn't have his seat belt on."

Good Cop took the softer approach. "How much alcohol did you say you had, sir?"

"I didn't, I'm not drunk. I just lost control of the car. It happens. Right now, all I care about is the kid. I want to speak to him."

"Maybe after *we've* finished talking," said Bad Cop.

Then a camera flashed, startling Santiago and causing him to drop the plastic cup.

The English photographer had worked hard to get the photo, trailing halfway around Madrid on his Lambretta before finally tracking down his victim.

Santiago snapped. "You scumbag!"

He leaped to his feet and launched himself at the photographer, landing one heavy punch to his face before being dragged back by both police officers.

"Señor Muñez, I am placing you under arrest," said Good Cop as he pulled the handcuffs from his belt.

The photographer hauled himself off the floor, wiping blood from his mouth as he checked that his precious camera was undamaged. It was fine, and the photographer wasn't thinking of retaliatory punches— his retaliation would be a million times better and a lot more lucrative.

The camera flashed repeatedly as Santiago was bundled down the corridor.

"See you in court, Santi!" grinned the delighted and suddenly much wealthier photographer, licking away the blood on his lips.

The police officers pulled Santi to a standstill for a moment while they secured the handcuffs.

And in that moment, he saw her.

His mother. For the first time in years. As Santi was about to be dragged away, the elevator doors opened and she was there, looking scared and bewildered.

She saw Santiago and their eyes met and Rosa-Maria froze, feeling an icy chill flood through her body as they stared at each other. Santiago almost burst into tears. Now. After all this time. He was so close to her now, at last. And he was about to be led away in shame.

He wanted to call out to her, but no words would come. And then he was bundled away, lost from his mother's sight. Again.

Rosa-Maria closed her eyes tightly as the tears welled up against her eyelids.

26

THE NIGHTMARE WASN'T OVER. Not by a long shot.

Santiago was driven to a police station, where the formalities of being charged were completed.

He watched as his possessions were listed and placed in a bag, he obeyed every instruction as his fingerprints were taken, and he stared passively as his mug-shot photographs were captured, front and profile. It felt even worse than being photographed by the leering, English paparazzi man.

Just before Santiago was led away to spend the remainder of the night in the cells, he was given the opportunity to make a single phone call.

Suddenly he felt completely alone. He didn't know who to call. Here he was, a famous footballer known throughout Spain and Europe, and there was no one he could instantly turn to.

Gavin would still be out celebrating and be in no condition to come to his aid. He couldn't put Roz or his family through any more torment. There was no one at the club who would react with sympathy to his latest misdemeanor.

He finally realized there was only one person he could call. He picked up the telephone, punched in the number, and listened to the ringing tone.

"Come on, pick up. Please, pick up."

Eventually, the call was answered. The voice was quiet, and the Geordie accent was unmistakable.

"Hello?"

"Glen, it's me. I'm sorry for calling so late, but I couldn't think of anyone else."

In the darkness of his bedroom in Newcastle, Glen glanced at the clock at his bedside. It was after three A.M., and Glen was not in the mood for an early morning catch-up call, especially from someone who had so recently fired him.

"I'm flattered," he said with more than a hint of sarcasm.

"I need your help, man. I've really messed up this time and I'm in a lot of trouble."

"What is it now?"

"My car's a wreck, Glen, and I hit a photographer; he was goading me. I've been arrested. The press are gonna have a field day over this, trashing my life."

Glen sighed. "Sounds to me like you're well able to do that for yourself without needing any help from the papers."

"Everything I touch has gone wrong, Glen."

"I'm not your agent anymore, Santiago, remember?"

"I'm sorry, man, I just feel like I keep screwing up and hurting everyone, and—"

"Don't apologize to me," said Glen, interrupting. "Save it for those who need it."

Glen was angry. And hurt. But he wasn't going to let Santiago know about the hurt he was feeling; he had too much pride in himself for that.

He let his words sink in for a moment before continuing.

"You're not a kid anymore, you're a grown man. You've earned a lot of praise on the pitch; it's time to earn some respect in the real world. Where it matters."

Glen couldn't see the tears running down Santi's face, but even if he had, he would have ended the conversation in the same way.

"Until you've done that, son, you're on your own. Good night."

It felt as though he had slept for little more than a few minutes, huddled uncomfortably on a small hard bed in the dark, cramped cell.

Santiago felt himself being shaken, none too gently, by the shoulder. He opened his eyes to see the Real player liaison director, Leo Vegaz, staring down at him.

He handed Santi a pair of sunglasses. "You're going to need these."

They emerged from the police station into a rainy Madrid morning and a hail of flashing cameras as the paparazzi continued with Santi's total humiliation.

"Say nothing," said Leo as journalists crowded around and fired off questions. He hurried Santi into the back of a waiting vehicle and as they drove away, he handed him the bag containing his possessions.

And then he gave him just one of the many newspapers lying on the seat between them.

Santi was front-page news. The mangled wreckage of his car was pictured in full color and the accompanying article didn't make good reading.

And it wasn't over when he got home. The paparazzi camped out by the front gates of the house throughout that day, and the next, making Santiago feel like a caged animal.

All the while, Glen's stinging words came back to haunt him. *"You're not a kid anymore. It's time to earn some respect."*

He was right. Santiago knew things had to change. But nothing *could* change until he had finally come to terms with the situation that had invaded almost every waking moment and most of his dreams for the past few months.

He knew he had to confront Rosa-Maria. Face-to-face.

But things were about to get even worse for Santi.

High-profile Premiership players who move to Spain are always a target for the paparazzi, and even an innocent moment can look totally different by the time the photographs make it to the tabloids or the glossy magazines.

Maybe Santiago should have remembered that when Jordana kissed him as they stood by her white Lamborghini outside the Buddha Bar. Even though that had been weeks earlier, long before Christmas, the photographs had only just appeared in the pages of *Heat* magazine.

That moment had been innocent, even though the events of New Year's Eve were not. But it was the kiss outside the Buddha that was finally to prove too much for Roz when she saw the photos.

The headline didn't help either:

SUPER SUB SCORES AWAY FROM HOME!

One of Roz's friends at work had given her the magazine, but not out of malice; she just wanted Roz to know before the gossip started spreading around the hospital.

Santiago was delighted when he looked at his cell and saw that the incoming call was from Roz. But the delight didn't last for long.

"How *could* you! You didn't even have the sense to do it in private; you had to flaunt it in front of the whole world!"

"What?" said Santi into his phone. "What are you talking about, Roz?"

"About *you*! And *her*! You're in all the magazines, Santi, with that . . . *woman*!"

"Magazine? What woman?"

"Oh! So how many have there been? Is she the real reason you couldn't come home at Christmas? How long has this been going on?"

Santiago realized that Roz had to be talking about the kiss outside the Buddha; he remembered the cameras flashing. "Baby, you're getting it all wrong. The press twists all that stuff."

"I can *see* it here in front of me, Santiago; I can *see* what you've been doing. Stop lying."

"But I'm not!"

Roz wasn't going to be convinced. "If that's the type of girl you want, then fine, Santi, you can have her."

"Look, I'm sorry, Roz," said Santiago desperately. "Things are all messed up right now."

"You've made a fool of me, and I don't deserve it!" shouted Roz. "I *knew* this would happen."

And then she hung up.

27

GAVIN KNEW FULL WELL that very few footballers could do like Teddy Sheringham of West Ham United and play at the highest level until the age of forty.

For most players, when they reach thirty, they discover that the clock seems to be ticking more loudly and that the football seasons pass more swiftly. Gavin had passed that milestone, and with it had come the realization that he wanted to prolong his career for as long as possible.

So he continued to work furiously in training, and it was paying off. And it wasn't just the training; he was also moderating his wild lifestyle—not completely, but significantly. There were fewer late nights out clubbing, he cut back on the booze, and he paid serious attention to his diet.

As Real moved on to the semifinal of the Champions League, he was the outstanding player and the goals came often.

"Goals are like buses," he told Santiago. "You wait for ages for one to come along . . ."

"And then three or four arrive together," said Santiago, finishing off the old cliché.

Santiago was also making good progress, and Gavin was there to support and encourage him as the plaster cast on his leg was removed and he took his first, tentative steps back to full fitness.

There were long sessions just walking on the treadmill and hours in the aqua-therapy pool and with the physical therapist. But slowly and steadily the strength came back and at last he was able to join the rest of the squad in training.

The season was proving a difficult one for Real, despite their progress in getting to the Champions League semifinal.

In a move that shocked the entire football world, club president Florentino Pérez announced his resignation and was replaced by Fernando Martín. The new man hinted that the era of the *galácticos* might be coming to an end.

He warned all the players that he expected hard work and effort in training and on the field, urging them to make him, the club, and the supporters proud.

No one took the words more to heart than Gavin, and as Santiago got back in shape, he, too, set out to prove to the new president, and to his coach, that Real's investment had, after all, been a wise one.

Van Der Merwe and his assistant, Steve McManaman, watched him closely during training, and when Santiago scored a fine goal in a practice match, the head coach was satisfied enough to consider him for selection.

But he had to be eased back in slowly; this time Van Der Merwe was not going to be rushed into another wrong decision.

Santi made a couple of brief but encouraging appearances from the bench in league fixtures but he sat out the first leg of the Champions League semifinal.

The surprise opponents were Olympique Lyon from France—not one of the biggest names in European football. But under ex-Liverpool boss Gérard Houllier, they were storming away with the French league and had waged an impressive Champions League campaign.

In the first leg in France, Real held out for a nil–nil draw. It meant they only needed to snatch a single goal and then defend in numbers at the Bernabéu to make the final.

But safety-first football was not the way Van Der Merwe operated. And neither did his players.

28

Rudi Der Merwe wanted any team he selected to play attacking football, to play the beautiful game as it should be played.

And as the whistle sounded for the kickoff to the second leg, that's exactly what he was expecting.

Santiago's impressive cameo appearances in the league matches had earned him a place on the bench. Van Der Merwe had not considered including him in the starting lineup; he was not yet fit enough for a full ninety minutes, and besides, Gavin's form fully justified his selection.

Van Der Merwe was starting with his strongest lineup, including the English center back, Jonathan Woodgate, who had suffered a cruel run of injuries since his move to Real.

The first minutes confirmed Van Der Merwe's belief in the positive, with his side playing attractive, attacking football, particularly up front where Gavin, Raúl, and Ronaldo were involved in some dazzling exchanges leading to a couple of outstanding saves by the Lyon keeper.

But there were no goals when Lyon won a free-kick in a dangerous position just outside the box.

Gavin took his place in the wall as the former Arsenal striker, Sylvain Wiltord, prepared to take the kick.

He struck it well and the ball flashed inches wide of the upright, temporarily silencing the Bernabéu faithful.

Real stuck to their attacking guns, forcing a series of spectacular saves from the Lyon keeper, who was having the game of his life.

Gavin was the unluckiest of all the Real forwards; by the time the match reached the hour mark he had been denied what had looked to be certain goals three times by the inspired keeper.

On the Real bench, Van Der Merwe was considering changes when, after a foul outside the Lyon box, Real was awarded a free-kick. Passions and tempers were running high and players from both sides rushed in to join the debate over the decision.

Gerard Houllier stood glum-faced on the touch-line. The free-kick was in perfect David Beckham territory, and the Frenchman was fully aware of the damage the Englishman could inflict from that range.

Beckham placed the ball deliberately. He was just to the left and seven or eight yards outside the penalty area. A three-man wall shifted from side to side, following the shouted orders of the Lyon keeper.

And then Beckham struck the free-kick. Virtually everyone in the stadium was expecting a curling shot, but the ball bent out wide, across the face of the goal.

Three Real players made their runs as the Lyon defense backpedaled furiously and the keeper moved anxiously across his goal line.

Gavin had timed his run to perfection. The speeding ball dropped and bounced once and he struck it viciously with his left foot. It was a sweet goal, the type players and coaches practice time after time on the training ground. And all that practice had made it work perfectly.

Gavin had done it again. The man who didn't score for seventeen matches was now scoring at a rate of almost a goal a game.

There were no complaints when the substitution board went up a couple of minutes later and Gavin saw he was being taken off and that Santiago was coming on. Gavin had done his job; he deserved a rest.

As Lyon pressed for an equalizer, Santi was swiftly up with the pace of the game. He had to be; after his long layoff he was desperate to be part of the big-time action again.

He collected a sweet pass from Roberto Carlos and with a dazzling display of trickery he left two Lyon defenders for dead, before a shot across goal that was just wide of the upright.

The Madridistas roared their approval, acknowledging with their whistles and cheers what they had been missing during the long months of Santi's absence.

Soon after, from the deftest of back-heels from Ronaldo, Santi, with his back to goal, wrong-footed the entire Lyon back line with a sweet, touch, and turn.

He had a sight of goal; he'd made the chance for himself and he was going to take it. As two Lyon defenders turned to give chase, Santi took two strides, lifted his head, and then struck the ball venomously. The diving keeper had no chance as the ball flashed by and the net bulged.

As the Bernabéu erupted with joy, Santi went hurtling toward the crowd, arms raised. Every one of his teammates ran in ecstatic pursuit and on the touchline, Van Der Merwe, Macca, and the entire Real bench were punching the air in delight.

Real was two up. Real was almost in the final of the Champions League.

Lyon threw everyone forward in the final few minutes, but the Real defense, marshaled superbly by Woodgate, hung on until, after one hundred and twenty long seconds of added time, the whistle sounded for the end of the match.

Real had done it! They were there. In the final of the Champions League, where they would meet the British Premiership club, Arsenal.

The postmatch television interviews were well under way, and Gavin stood patiently in the corridor leading from the dressing room giving the routine answers to the routine questions footballers receive after a big match victory.

"It was touch and go out there," said the British television interviewer, stating the obvious before thrusting the microphone toward Gavin's face.

Gavin was all smiles, elated at the way his season had turned around. He couldn't resist answering with every footballing cliché he could remember. "Yeah, well, they had us pinned down for the first forty-five minutes but those Lyon boys will be sick as parrots 'cause it's a game of two halves and it ain't over 'til the fat lady sings. That's football."

The interviewer's next question wiped the smile off Gavin's face.

"Do you think you'll play in the final or do you think that the coach will choose Santiago instead?"

Before Gavin could think of the words to answer, the massed microphones and cameras swung across to Santiago.

"Santiago, you got Real Madrid into the final. Can you tell us how you feel?"

Santi was ready with the diplomatic, team-first answers. "I'm just glad we made it through to the final. It was a great team effort."

Another interviewer fired in a question.

"Everyone knows that you and Gavin are buddies. This must be putting a lot of pressure on your friendship."

Santiago glanced over at his friend before answering. "Look, we're part of a team. But first, we're friends."

29

SANTI STOOD at an upstairs window of his huge mansion and peered down at the massed hordes of paparazzi camped outside the front gate.

Real's progress to the Champions League final had only increased the media obsession with the lives of the star players, and particularly of Santiago Muñez.

He had been big news on and off the pitch ever since his arrival in Madrid, and with the final fast approaching, the so called "gentlemen of the press" knew that big money was there to be made if the slightest indiscretion or the merest hint of further scandal could be captured on camera.

Santi was still desperate to try to track down his mother, Rosa-Maria, but apart from when he was at training he had been a virtual prisoner in his own home. At this rate, he would never find her.

He glanced down into the garden and saw one of the men he'd employed to tend the grounds he never went on for fear of a cameraman popping his head over the wall.

And then Santi smiled. He had an idea.

The lurking paparazzi had no idea that Santiago had even left the house when he was driven away from the rear gate, sitting between two gardeners in the back of a truck.

Santiago almost laughed at the irony of it. For years he had done exactly this every day as he scratched out a living as a gardener to the rich of L.A. with his father, Herman. He had stared enviously at the mansions and the manicured gardens as he raked leaves and trimmed lawns.

Now he was rich—he had it all—but at this moment it felt as though he had nothing.

The search had to begin somewhere, so he went back to the area where Enrique had jumped from the car and gone running off with his sports bag at the end of their first meeting.

Santiago carried Rosa-Maria's photograph with him. He went into cafés and stopped people on the street, showing the photograph, asking if anyone knew her or where she might be. He got nothing in return but shrugs and shakes of the head.

Madrid was a big city. She could be anywhere.

He tried again the following day, moving from street to street, district to district. Eventually he met a couple of hard-looking young guys on the corner of a street. They were obviously not football fans, as neither of them recognized Santi as he took out the photograph and asked them if they knew the woman.

They were sizing up Santiago warily, looking at him more than at the photograph.

"You don't look like police," said one of them at last.

"I'm not," said Santi quickly. "I just need to find her."

Reassured, they looked at the photo again.

"I might know where she works," said the second guy.

"Really?" said Santi, feeling his heart start to pound. "Where?"

The young guy shrugged his shoulders; there was still some bargaining to be done and Santiago was wearing an expensive Rolex on his wrist.

The young guy nodded down at the Rolex. "That's a nice watch."

It was early evening when Santi stepped from the taxi and stared across at the small bar on the far side of the road. He didn't know the exact time; he no longer had a watch.

Nervously he walked across the road, pushed open the door, and went inside. It was busy, and noisy, but the chatter stopped completely almost as soon as the first person recognized Santiago.

Within seconds everyone had stopped drinking and speaking and was staring in disbelief at the sight of the famous Real Madrid player who had appeared in their midst from nowhere.

Rosa-Maria was behind the bar, concentrating on the drink she was pouring. She suddenly became aware of the silence and looked up to see Santiago standing perfectly still, halfway across the room.

Her eyes widened, her mouth fell open, and everyone in the room watched as she whispered one word, "Santiago."

Miguel was also behind the bar, as confused as his customers while mother and son stared at each other but said nothing.

Slowly Rosa-Maria walked from behind the bar and went to her son. She stopped in front of him, her eyes fixed on his as if she were searching to discover everything she had never known about the many long years of his life she had missed.

She raised her right hand, going to touch his check,

but then snatched it away as if she were afraid that if she touched him he might disappear.

But Santiago caught her hand in his. He held it firmly, scared now to let go.

And then, without either of them knowing how it happened, they were hugging, holding each other so tightly, tears filling their eyes.

The customers in the bar stared at one another, bewildered and slightly embarrassed at the very private and intensely personal scene they were witnessing.

Miguel was the first one to speak, not quite certain why he decided to empty the bar, but knowing that somehow it was the right thing to do. "Right, closing time, drink up everyone." There were a few halfhearted mutters of complaint, but Miguel had made up his mind. "Early night tonight, we'll see you all tomorrow."

30

THERE WAS SO MUCH TO SAY, so much to learn, but now that the moment had finally come they were both struggling to find the words. They were sitting at a table in one corner of the bar, speaking hesitantly and haltingly.

Miguel was behind the bar, cleaning glasses and occasionally darting quick looks in their direction. He had asked his wife little and his mind was tumbling with the few words of explanation she had offered. They, too, had much to discuss, but it could wait. For now.

Santi had to ask the questions that had been burning him up for so long. "Why did you go? Why did you leave us?"

Rosa-Maria looked nervously at her son, knowing that her confession had to be made.

"It's . . . it's hard to explain. It had nothing to do with you."

"It had everything to do with us," said Santiago almost angrily.

Rosa-Maria nodded. Her story was difficult to tell, but she knew that if she and Santi were going to attempt to build a relationship, it had to be told.

"I abandoned you. I . . . I was walking home one night and . . . and two men attacked me. One of them was . . . he was your uncle. I managed to get home, but I knew then that I could never tell your father what happened."

Santi could see the pain in his mother's eyes as the memories returned.

"And I panicked, and I ran away."

Santi's mind was churning. "But never even a call? Nothing."

"Santiago," said Rosa-Maria defiantly, "I came back three weeks later, and you were all gone. And no one could tell me where my family had disappeared to. And those who could, wouldn't. Then I found out it was too late; you had left Mexico."

She glanced across at her husband, Miguel, and then looked back at Santiago.

"When I saw you on the television I wanted to get in touch with you so much, but I was sure that you wished me dead."

Santi reached out and took his mother's hand again. "How could you think that? I was angry. My dad was angry. He died full of anger. At you, at everything, at the world."

His words were almost as difficult for Rosa to take as her own story had been to tell.

"He loved you very much," said Santi.

Tears filled Rosa-Maria's eyes again. "I'm . . . I'm . . ." She leaned forward and kissed Santi's hands. "Forgive me."

Santi nodded. "Everything's going to be okay," he said softly. "You'll see."

The sun had set over the towering billboards—one showing Real Madrid's new star, Santiago Muñez—but the kids were determined to continue with their football match until it was too dark to see.

Enrique wasn't letting the cast on his arm or the cuts and bruises on his face stop him from throwing everything into the game, especially as the bullying Tito was on the opposing side.

A small girl was running up and down at the edge of the makeshift field, hardly involved in the action, particularly when the larger boys came thundering in her direction.

She stopped running when she saw the two figures approaching. And then she stared.

"Enrique!"

Enrique had the ball—he didn't want to lose it—but the girl shouted again urgently.

"Enrique!"

The ball rolled away as Enrique looked up and everyone's eyes followed the girl's pointing finger.

Rosa-Maria was walking toward them—with Santiago.

"Hey, bro," he said as he reached Enrique. "You want a game?"

Enrique beamed and nodded, for once lost for words. But his joy was made complete a few minutes later as Santiago effortlessly avoided a lunging tackle from Tito and casually knocked the bully to the ground, leaving him sprawled facedown, eating dirt.

Santiago's other brother, Julio, was at home in L.A., playing a game on his computer when a new window opened on his screen to inform him that he had e-mail.

He went to his mailbox, saw that the e-mail was from Santi, and read the few brief lines of explanation. Quickly he began to download the attachment.

"Grandma," he called. "Mail from Santi."

Mercedes came in from the kitchen. She stood behind Julio and together they watched a photograph gradually appear on the screen.

It was Santi, with Enrique and Rosa-Maria. They were smiling, self-consciously but happily, and Mercedes could see for herself the pride and delight in her older grandson's face. She had been so afraid that if he found his mother there would be more pain and heartache.

But the photograph told the story. Santiago looked so happy.

Mercedes sighed as she thought of her own son, Herman. He had never forgiven Rosa-Maria for deserting them, and neither had she. But nothing could change what had happened in the past and as she stared at the photograph, Mercedes realized that what mattered most now was the future. It was time to move on.

She squeezed Julio's shoulders and smiled as he turned and looked up at her.

"Your mother," she said. "Now we must do something about you meeting her, too."

Roz was sitting in the darkness. She was perched on the bottom stair of the house in Newcastle struggling to hold back the tears as she played Santiago's phone message for a second time.

"It's good you're out. This way I can say what I need to say. Everything has turned inside out since I came here. The money, the fame, without you it's nothing, Roz."

Roz could hear that Santi was struggling to get the words right as he hesitated.

"I finally met my mother. Not knowing was tearing me apart. It's still hard to take in, but I think things might be okay. It's going to take time."

He paused again and Roz pictured him in Madrid as he made the call.

"I'm not going to make any more excuses for what I've done. All I can say is I'm just so sorry for treating you the way I have, for pushing you away. I've been a total jerk."

Roz smiled. He was right about that. He'd been stupid, irresponsible, selfish, and, just like he said, a total jerk.

But there were things that Roz wanted to say to Santiago, too. Things that she'd never had the chance to discuss with him before their world had so completely and dramatically fallen apart.

She looked down at her stomach and marveled again at the swelling that seemed to increase slightly almost every day. She was almost six months pregnant. Santiago didn't even know that he was going to become a father.

"I want to make things right," he said, nearing the end of his message. "Please call me. Let me know if you'll give me a second chance. I love you, Roz."

31

THE BUILDUP to the Champions League final sparked unprecedented levels of debate and speculation in the press and media: Harris or Muñez, who was it to be?

Gavin had been playing well and was scoring again. But Santiago was a proven match winner, and despite his off-the-field antics, what mattered most to everyone was that Real won the match.

Van Der Merwe was on the telephone in his office when Santiago came in looking as though he was spoiling for a fight.

"I'll have to call you back," said Van Der Merwe into the phone before hanging up.

"What is it?" he said, looking up at Santi.

"Are you going to start me?" demanded Santiago firmly. "In the final?"

Van Der Merwe sighed with irritation. "I seem to remember us doing this dance once before. Don't you?"

Santiago stared hard at the coach. "Play Gavin."

"What?" said Van Der Merwe, taken aback. "Is this some kind of game, Muñez?"

"No, boss," said Santiago. "I just want to ask you to keep me on the bench. Start Gavino. If he plays well in the final he could still make the England World Cup squad."

Van Der Merwe shook his head. One minute Muñez was telling him to start him on the team and the next he was asking him to leave him out.

"I love football," said Santiago before his coach had a chance to speak. "But without my friends and my family, it's not enough. When I came here I was . . . dazzled by it all; I lost sight of what was important and did my best to throw everything away."

"Muñez—"

"Let me finish, please, boss," said Santi urgently. "Gavin's been with me all the way. He's my *friend*. And while I've been running around like an idiot, he's been working hard and earning his place. But he's running out of time and he can't finish this season on the bench."

Santiago let out a long breath. "That's all I'm asking, boss." He turned to go.

"Muñez?"

"Boss?" said Santi, turning back.

"I pick the team."

32

MIGUEL SLID THE KEY into the lock of the entrance door to the bar, watched by Rosa-Maria and Enrique. He turned the heavy old key, pulled it from the lock, and then rattled the door handle to check that the door was actually secured as Enrique waited impatiently and his mother just smiled.

Across the street stood a gleaming Audi. A well-dressed driver was waiting to open the doors for his VIP passengers.

They crossed the road and the driver smiled at them as he pulled open one of the rear doors. On the backseat were flowers for Rosa-Maria and three Real Madrid shirts, each bearing the name Muñez. Santiago's newly found family was on their way to watch the final of the Champions League.

His other family—grandmother Mercedes and brother Julio—was ready, with what seemed to have developed into the L.A. branch of the Real Madrid supporters' club crammed into the living room of their house. Mercedes was, as always, in the seat of honor closest to the television screen, and Julio was at her side.

Roz was at home in Newcastle, with only her mom, Carol, for company. Roz had to see the final, but in her condition the safest place to do so was from the comfort of an armchair. She, too, was staring at the television as pundits made their prematch forecasts and predicted a close but exciting final.

Glen had chosen to watch the match in a Newcastle pub, along with some of the staff from his garage. If things had worked out differently he would have been there, close to the action, giving Santi support and words of encouragement before taking his reserved seat in one of the executive boxes.

But things hadn't worked out differently, and all Glen could do now was watch from afar, like hundreds of thousands of other football fans all around the globe.

The Bernabéu had been selected as the venue for the Champions League final long before the competition got under way.

It was the luck of the draw as far as Real Madrid was concerned, but Arsenal, too, would feel at home with their fans filling half the stadium.

Arsène Wenger had performed near miracles in getting the team he was patiently rebuilding to the final. Many of his stalwarts had either moved on, as in the case of Patrick Vieira, or were suffering from long-term injuries.

But the Arsenal injury crisis had meant the emergence of several new young stars including the dynamic and feisty English midfielder, T. J. Harper.

The Real players sat nervously on the benches in the dressing room, waiting patiently for Van Der Merwe to begin his prematch talk.

Van Der Merwe smiled. "I have taken you as far as I can, to base camp." He paused for a moment and then nodded toward the door. "Out there, that's Everest."

A few of the players nodded their appreciation at his words.

"The legends are watching you: Di Stéfano, Butragueño, Sánchez. Remember them, and remember you deserve to be here. To make history. As a team. You are one step away from the ultimate achievement, the biggest prize in club football."

He held up his team sheet, knowing by heart every

name he had written down without needing to refer to his notes, and began to reveal his starting lineup.

"Casillas. Salgado. Woodgate. Helguera. Carlos." He paused. Everyone was staring intently. "Zidane, Beckham, Guti, Robinho. Ronaldo."

Real's hugely popular skipper, Raúl, had been injured in the buildup to the final and was not fit enough to start the match. Only one place remained. Van Der Merwe locked eyes with Santiago as he said the final name.

"Harris."

Gavin's eyes widened in surprise. He looked over at Santiago and saw that he was smiling at him, sharing his joy.

As the players filed from the dressing room, heading for the tunnel, their coach's final words of encouragement were still ringing in their ears.

"You made it. The Champions League final. I don't want you to forget why you're here, but I want you to play as if you have nothing to lose. Forget the money, forget the press, forget the cameras, forget everything. Enjoy."

The Real players came face-to-face with their opponents at the entrance to the tunnel. Many were old friends, old rivals, or, in some cases—old sparring partners.

The two teams began the long walk down the tunnel, hearing the tumultuous noise that was building toward its crescendo. As they emerged into the dazzling lights of the Bernabéu, the deafening sound ringing around the stadium reached a level that few had ever experienced.

They reached the center circle and formed the lineup for the UEFA anthem and then they began the traditional handshakes, with the Real players moving along the Arsenal ranks, nodding and offering a brief "good luck."

Henry, Bergkamp, Cole, Pires, Ljungberg. Even without the inspirational Patrick Vieira, Arsenal was still a team packed with potential match winners. And apart from the established stars, they also had T. J. Harper, their new young superstar with the looks and confidence of a rapper or movie star.

David Beckham shook his hand and nodded. "T. J. Good luck."

Harper smiled broadly and then glanced toward Gavin, who was next in line.

"Ain't me who's gonna need the luck, bro," said Harper to Beckham.

As Gavin took Harper's hand, the Arsenal player leaned in close and whispered something in his ear. The psychological games were beginning.

Gavin stood back and a look of anger flashed across his face. Harper walked away, laughing at drawing first blood in the battle of the minds. David Beckham put a hand on Gavin's shoulder; he knew all about opponents with windup tactics.

"Take no notice" was all he said. It was enough. Gavin smiled and nodded and then went jogging off to take up his starting position.

On the bench, Santiago exchanged an anxious look with Steve McManaman. They had both seen Gavin's furious look during the handshakes.

The referee checked with his assistants and then raised his whistle to his lips and the piercing shrill penetrated even the roar of eighty-five thousand voices.

The Champions League final was underway.

33

THE MATCH couldn't have gotten off to a worse start for Real—or for Gavin Harris.

In the very first minute, as he collected a short pass, he was robbed by the quick-thinking T. J. Harper, who set off on a run toward the Real goal.

Gavin turned to give chance and quickly made up ground. Just as Harper reached the box, Gavin made his tackle. It was well timed and clean, but Harper went down dramatically.

The referee came racing in, and as Gavin clambered to his feet, he heard the whistle sound and saw him pointing to the penalty spot.

There were looks and shouts of disbelief from the Real bench and from the Madridistas, but worse was to come.

The ref reached into his top pocket, and for a moment, Gavin's heart was in his mouth at the horrifying thought that he was about to suffer the same fate as Santiago had in the match against Valencia.

But the card was yellow. Gavin turned away, feeling relief but dismay, as well as anger toward Harper, who had at very best "earned" the spot kick.

The Arsenal midfielder had already grabbed the ball and placed it on the spot for the penalty. The Real supporters' jeers and whistles of derision were still ringing around the stadium as Harper prepared to take the kick.

It was perfectly placed, low and hard into the left corner, and although Casillas guessed correctly and dived the right way, the ball easily beat his outstretched arm.

Arsenal was a goal up after just one minute. And as Real tried to regroup and counter the early disaster, it quickly began to look as though the Premiership team would go further ahead. Their moves were quick and incisive and the Premiership-style pace was close to overwhelming the more measured buildup of Real.

Bergkamp was just wide with a rasping shot and Henry, darting through his favored left channel, went even closer with a header as Arsenal totally dominated.

The *galácticos* of Madrid were being outplayed and outthought as they struggled to overcome the set-back of losing a goal so early on.

On the bench, Santiago was living every move and feeling every tackle, desperately wanting to be part of the action, yet willing Gavin to make a special contribution to the final.

But it was all Arsenal. Freddie Lundberg was causing havoc on the left flank, twice bringing stunning saves from Casillas, who was undoubtedly Real's player of the first half.

Real was fortunate not to be further behind when the referee brought the first half to a close, and they trooped from the field looking bewildered and bemused. They needed to get back to the dressing room. To regroup. To recover.

As the players entered the tunnel, separated by the steel grill that divides the stairway, T. J. Harper decided to add to Gavin's frustration and fury.

"Oh, dear," he mocked. "We do look upset."

Gavin couldn't stop himself from slamming both hands against the steel. "You cheating, cocky—!"

Steve McManaman was just behind Gavin. He pulled him away. "Leave it, Gav! He's not worth it!"

Once the Real players had settled onto the benches in the dressing room, Van Der Merwe began his halftime team talk by kicking the tactics board. It clattered to the floor. No one said a word, but Macca decided to do the diplomatic thing by picking up the board. He was rewarded with a glare from the coach.

Van Der Merwe turned to Gavin. "Harris!"

It was the moment Gavin had dreaded ever since his booking. He was being taken off.

"Harper made you look like an idiot!"

"I know, boss. But please, just give me—"

He didn't get the chance to finish.

"I want to push you forward. I'm bringing on Santi, he'll play in behind."

Gavin breathed a huge sigh of relief. He'd been reprieved, and Santiago was coming on to add to the Real firepower.

Van Der Merwe spent the remainder of the interval reminding his players how they had allowed Arsenal to dominate and even intimidate them during the first period, and they went back out onto the field fired up with new energy and determination. They were one down, but great teams could come back from much greater deficits. And they *were* a great team. They had forty-five minutes to prove just how great they were.

34

As Santiago waited on the touchline for the referee's signal that he could join the second-half action, Van Der Merwe gave him a few last tactical instructions.

"Find Becks with some one-twos, wide on the left. They won't be expecting that."

Santi nodded, and as the referee beckoned him onto the field he knew that his mother and Enrique would be watching from their seats up in the executive box and that his grandmother and Julio would be glued to their TV set out in L.A.

And Santi knew that back in Newcastle, Glen and Roz would be watching, too. He had to play the half of his life, for all of them.

At the pub in Newcastle, the whole bar erupted in cheers and applause as they saw their former favorite sprint onto the field.

One of Glen's mechanics—the aptly nicknamed Foghorn, because of his booming voice—shouted his pleasure. "Here we go, lads, an injection of Geordie skill!"

He turned to Glen. "Your lad's gonna do the Toon proud, Glen."

Glen nodded and smiled with pride, but his whispered reply went unheard in the cheers and shouts of the packed bar. "He's not my lad anymore."

Santiago was quickly up with the pace of the game, and he followed his coach's instructions to the letter. In a sweet move he found Beckham wide on the left and was in the perfect position to receive the returning ball.

He back-heeled the ball to Gavin, who was following up at pace. He took the shot on the run from twenty-five yards out and it flashed just wide of an upright.

On the bench, Van Der Merwe nodded his satisfaction to Macca. This was better. Much better.

But Arsène Wenger was also absorbing the change in the Real tactics and was plotting his own changes. It was almost like a game of chess, with the two grand masters on opposing benches, deciding on their moves and adapting their tactics as the drama unfolded.

Santi, Gavin, and David Beckham, more used to the English style of play than most of their teammates, were beginning to cause Arsenal problems, and as the second half settled, Real looked as though they might yet be capable of inflicting some serious damage of their own.

But then Thierry Henry struck a demoralizing blow, demonstrating yet again why he is the most feared and most coveted striker in the English Premiership.

He collected a pass close to the halfway line, and then set off on a mazy, electrifying run.

He left two defenders in his wake and approached the box through the left channel. Casillas came charging out to meet him, but as a third Real defender made a despairing tackle, the Frenchman fired the ball hard and low across the diving keeper.

Henry was already racing away in triumph as the Arsenal supporters began to celebrate a classic goal.

Real was two down and looking as though they were down and out.

As the minutes ticked by, and Real threw everything into all-out attack, Arsenal came agonizingly close to adding to their tally on more than one occasion.

Both managers made changes, but far from switching to all-out defense, the Gunners continued to press and probe and push for the third goal. Henry was inspirational, outshining even his fellow Frenchman, Zidane, who was doing everything he could to drag Real back into the match.

Real was still playing football, but it was increasingly desperate football.

Thomas Gravesen had come on to add some steel to the Real midfield, but still Arsenal was dominant, and with only seven minutes to go, there seemed to be no possible way back.

Henry collected the ball just outside the box. He jinked one way, and then the other, wrong-footing Jonathan Woodgate, and then found Freddie Lundberg, who came sprinting into the area.

As he hurtled across the box and shaped to shoot, Roberto Carlos tore across the area, clattering in with a sliding tackle that brought the Swede crashing to the ground.

This time there was no debate, no arguing. It was a definite penalty.

T. J. Harper looked to be the coolest person in the stadium as he carefully placed the ball on the spot for his second penalty.

The Bernabéu went silent.

Up in the executive box, Rosa-Maria clasped Enrique's hand. In L.A., Mercedes was doing exactly the same with her grandson, Julio. In Newcastle, Roz reached out and took her mother's hand, and in the city center pub, Glen clenched his fists. Even Foghorn was silent.

The Real keeper, Casillas, steadied himself, leaving

his decision on which way to dive until Harper started his run-up. Whichever way he went, it could only be a calculated guess.

The Arsenal and Real players hovered at the edge of the box, waiting to pounce or try to clear should the ball be saved and bounce back into play.

But Harper had no intention of letting the ball finish up anywhere but in the back of the net.

He began his run-up and Casillas made his decision. Harper hit the ball hard and high toward the top right corner. Casillas had guessed correctly. He leaped across his goal line, arms at full stretch, and he felt the ball thud against his fingers and onto the crossbar.

It spun into the air and as it dropped, Santiago was quickest to react, even quicker than Harper, who ran in to challenge. Santi swiveled and hoofed the ball as hard and as high as he could, into the Arsenal half.

It soared away, skyward, leaving many of the players rooted to the spot, just watching.

But Gavin was off and running, tearing up the field as he followed the flight of the ball.

It was one on one: Gavin versus the Arsenal keeper, Lehmann. They were charging toward each other like express trains, looking as though they were hurtling into an unstoppable, head-on collision.

Gavin watched the ball as it dropped. He could hear Lehmann thundering toward him. But he never took his eyes off the ball.

There wasn't time to let it bounce; he had to hit it on the volley. He unleashed his shot with all the venom he could muster.

Lehmann could do nothing to stop it. The ball passed him like a missile and he could only look back in disbelief as it rocketed into the net.

Gavin didn't stop to celebrate. He followed the ball into the goal, grabbed it, and went tearing back toward the center spot.

There was still a chance. Just.

35

THERE WERE FOUR minutes remaining. Four minutes for Real to try to force the match into extra time.

Arsenal had given up all thought of attacking football. Now it was their turn for desperate defense.

But Real was suddenly a team inspired, suddenly, in the very last moments, playing football worthy at last of the Real of old.

Zidane threaded the ball to Ronaldo, who found David Beckham out wide. He slid a measured pass through to Gavin, who was in position to shoot again. That was what the Arsenal defense were expecting, but Gavin cleverly sent across a long pass, which sat up invitingly for Santiago.

His first-time shot thundered back off the crossbar, and all around the stadium there were groans of despair and frustration.

But the attack was still alive, with Gavin and Beckham urging their teammates on with clenched fists and snarls of encouragement.

A lunging tackle earned the Gunners a few seconds' respite from the onslaught, but more importantly for Real, it gave them a corner.

Beckham went to the corner flag to place the ball, and on the bench, Van Der Merwe and McManaman checked their watches yet again.

The corner sailed over, deep into the heart of the penalty box, swinging away from the keeper, but he bravely raced from his line and punched it away.

The forty-five minutes were up. Arsène Wenger was on his feet, glaring at the fourth official and pointing toward his watch.

But there were two minutes of additional time to be added.

Still two minutes for Real to grab an equalizer.

Lehmann's punched clearance had only been half-cleared. After a midfield tussle, Roberto Carlos intercepted the ball as it bounced free. It was all-out attack now. It had to be. He ran at the Arsenal defense, dragging two players with him toward the corner flag.

Before either of them could make the tackle, the Brazilian thumped in a cross. Santiago was on the edge of the box. He knew for certain that the ball was going to drop for him, he knew for certain he was going to volley it home.

He did.

Lehmann hardly saw it and had no chance to stop it.

Everyone in the stadium and millions of television viewers around the world could barely believe what they were witnessing. This was a comeback to compare with the great comebacks in footballing history.

The Arsenal players were stunned and staring at each other. How could it have happened? The trophy had been theirs, it had been almost in touching distance, but now the dreaded specter of extra time hovered over them.

And the momentum was all with Real.

The Madridistas were still screaming their delight as Arsenal restarted the game. But they were in disarray, they lost possession, and the ball was with Real once again.

Guti threaded it through to Gavin and he swept it imperiously on to Santi who saw another shooting chance. He shaped for the shot but a despairing lunge from T. J. Harper brought him down and the referee blew for a free-kick.

The two additional minutes were virtually up and the Arsenal players crowded around the ref, urging him to blow for full time.

But David Beckham already had the ball.

He calmly placed it for the free-kick and the Arsenal defenders hurriedly took their positions in the wall, following the barked instructions of Lehmann.

The free-kick was in exactly the right sort of range for a Beckham specialty dead-ball attempt, and at just the right angle to bend around a wall.

The Bernabéu went silent.

In L.A. Santiago's grandmother mouthed a silent prayer and, up in the stands, his mother did the same thing.

Santiago watched, Gavin watched, it seemed as though the whole world was watching, as Beckham rocked back on his left foot for a moment before beginning his run-up.

He struck it perfectly, even more perfectly than the legendary free-kick he had struck for England against Greece.

The Arsenal defenders leaped high to try to intercept, but the ball arced over their heads and curled into the top corner, past the outstretched hands of the diving Lehmann.

The Bernabéu erupted as Beckham wheeled away in triumph and the final whistle sounded. Miraculously, almost unbelievably, there would be no need for extra time.

As Beckham turned back, Gavin and Santiago were there. They leaped into each other's arms, screaming their joy and basking in the tumultuous adoration of the Madridistas.

The three goal scorers were together.

Champions of Europe.